Published by
Merit Press
an imprint of F+W Media, Inc.
10151 Carver Road, Suite 200
Blue Ash, OH 45242. U.S.A.
www.meritpressbooks.com

ISBN 10: 1-4405-8460-5
ISBN 13: 978-1-4405-8460-2
eISBN 10: 1-4405-8461-3
eISBN 13: 978-1-4405-8461-9

Printed in the United States of America.

10 9 8 7 6 5 4 3 2 1

Cover design by Sylvia McArdle.
Cover images © iStockphoto.com/logosstock; kurtvate,
avid Schrader, donatas1205, Sergei Uriadnikov, scusi/123RF.

This book is available at quantity discounts for bulk purchases.
For information, please call 1-800-289-0963.

WHO
MACKIE S

Lin Ka

This book, c
pu

Merit Pr

Dedication

With appreciation for the professionals and volunteers who work to rehabilitate sick and injured wild animals.

Acknowledgments

I feel fortunate to have Jacquelyn Mitchard as my Merit Press editor. When an author/editor of Ms. Mitchard's caliber gives you the nod, optimism about life in general soars. I also thank Sam Bardelson for his early editing insights, and test readers who offered feedback or professional expertise: Gavin Hollyer, Patrick Amo, Maddie Gander, Elena Fox, and Susanne Bardelson. Many thanks to Field's End, a writers' community, especially fellow authors Barbara Clarke, Margaret Nevinski, and Margaret Chang for their ongoing counsel and camaraderie. Special thanks to Tim Richards for keeping me strong with core training as I wrote *Who Is Mackie Spence?* Finally, I'm indebted to my enduring friends who encouraged me to publish, including wildlife photographer Dottie Tison and members of the No Guilt Book Club.

CHAPTER 1

Shifting restlessly in French class, I stare at Mackenzie Allison Spence, but not for the usual reasons. Sure, she has long, dark hair, mischief-flashing eyes, and curves as sweet as a well-placed ball on goal. But lately I've been trying to figure her out, which is odd because we've been friends since we were kids.

The big news about Mackie is that she almost drowned over summer break, when her family's boat capsized in a storm off Yaquina Bay in Oregon. Her parents and sister were rescued within twenty minutes. In the deep troughs of fifty-two-degree water, Mackie wasn't found for three hours and then she was in a coma for a week. A Coast Guard captain called her survival "one for the record books."

That was just a few months before we started our junior year. Soltrice Island, a fifteen-mile square piece of land in Puget Sound, has only one high school. It's a small place where everyone knows everyone. And it's the kind of place where it's nearly impossible to keep a secret for very long.

After she returned from near death in Oregon, I didn't see much of Mackie. So, it surprised me when she appeared one August afternoon at the Olympic Wildlife Shelter.

As part of my volunteer duties, I was cleaning the Large Flight Cage, a wood and wire structure built to give big, injured birds a place to relearn flying. Mackie arrived outside the cage with our volunteer coordinator. Because the shelter has a low-contact policy that forbids talking around the animals, I could only nod to her when she walked outside the enclosure. Mackie nodded back at me as her eyes searched the inside of the cage.

But Number 26, our mature female bald eagle in Large Cage rehab, had a bizarre reaction. She lit on a low perch, turned to Mackie, put her head down, and pulled her wings in. All signs of deep respect from an eagle. Mackie gave Number 26 a smile like she'd just bumped into an old friend. How was Number 26 an old friend? I tightened my lips to keep quiet.

Since then, I've been with Mackie for five work sessions, and every time, the mammals, birds, and even a turtle acted weird. It's like some pecking order kicks in and the animals calm down. An injured animal's natural response to humans is fright and flight. Not around Mackie. She gets respect, every time. *Very strange.*

I stretch my legs out under my low desktop, trying to get comfortable. That's not easy when you're sixteen years old and six foot one. How can Mackie sit so still? Maybe she's concentrating. I know a thing or two about needing to focus. I've always had trouble with reading, and my spelling isn't great either.

"Jeremy Tarleton, écoutez-vous?" Madame Purcell asks me.

Uh oh.

"Oui, Madame. Il regard les femmes et pose le question pour les garcons," I translate, fumbling for the words. Not good. French isn't my best class.

Mackie turns to me with a sympathetic grin. Her smile is sweet, but her eyes look sad. The sadness thing started after the accident, and seems to be getting worse.

When Mackie returned home after her near drowning, she didn't act like herself. She'd always been really friendly, with a laugh like she was being tickled. After the accident, her smile hasn't come as quickly, and she hasn't laughed as often, either. I asked Jen about it. Jen and Mackie have been close friends forever. Jen said we had to give Mackie more time to recover; that it must have been awful to be trapped in those huge waves, and then lost in a coma.

Also after the accident, Mackie stopped seeing Brody Cameron, All-State soccer forward, senior letterman, and self-appointed alpha. He acts like their break up is no big deal. But I think it's the first time that Brody has been dropped by a girl.

After French class, as I hurry to the locker room for cross-country team practice, I flash to Mackie's face when she first saw Number 26. Her eyes had opened, and she'd let out a happy sigh like it was some kind of a reunion. *How can Mackie and Number 26, our rehab eagle, know each other?*

In the locker room, Brody stands talking with a few of the guys.

"Hey," he says, as I set my gear bag on a nearby bench. His chin juts up for what passes as a smile from his cheerleader-magnet face. Brody's a senior, so he doesn't usually have much time for me. He signals for the others to go ahead without him.

Brody and I walk out of the gym building to the hot, dry grass on the practice field. He surprises me by chatting about our next meet. Finally he asks, "You see much of Mackie these days?"

"We have some classes together."

"Does she seem different lately?"

"She's been pretty quiet."

"Right. She's a real quiet one. She seeing anyone?" he asks, flexing his jaw muscles like a fish opening and closing its gills.

"I don't know. She's usually with the girls when we leave class."

"Huh. Jilly wants to hang with me. Might as well," Brody says, flicking a small stone aside with the toe of his shoe. Not particularly wanting to know more about Jilly and Brody's new relationship status, I offer no comment.

We move into our warm-up drill, and my focus shifts to Coach. He stares at James Spooner like Spooner is a piece of meat beyond its expiration date. Terrific. It doesn't take long for us to learn why. Spooner has been kicked off the team after failing our latest drug test.

After practice, I catch a ride home with our neighbor, Ben. Ben's a senior, on cross-country, and started giving me rides to school last

April. He's smart, and on track to graduate in late December. My dad says Ben will 'go places.'

Entering through our front door, I hurry past our family photos along the length of the hallway. In all of the pictures I have dark hair and wide, greenish-gray eyes. After my sixth birthday the photos show a wide crease at the outside corner of my left eye, a reminder that I'd tripped and fallen on a rake. My badass, gardening-tool scar.

In the kitchen, I find chaos. Mom is home from teaching ceramics. She stands at the stove stirring sauce in a pot and holds an unopened package of pasta in her other hand. She squints to read the small print on the back of the package. Justin, my twelve-year-old brother, leans against the counter. He's been using our salad spinner as a launch pad. Lettuce is all over the place.

"Justin," Mom says, "you're not being helpful. I want you to re-wash the lettuce and close the top of the spinner this time. Jeremy, would you please put the food in those grocery bags in the pantry?" Her rapidly blinking eyes show me she's in a no-nonsense mood. I don't have to ask what kind of day she's had at school.

I set my backpack on a chair and give Justin a goofy grin. He nods his head and begins to collect the scattered greens.

"How was practice?" Mom asks, as she dumps the pasta into some boiling water.

"Coach cut Spooner from the team," I say, lifting a bag of groceries off the counter while inhaling the aroma of fennel-seasoned sauce. Mom's pasta sauce is the best.

"Why?"

"He tested positive. Ethan will probably move up."

"Spooner has had problems for a long time. Maybe this will be a good thing for him."

"Maybe, but Ethan's not as fast as Spooner."

"Don't give up on Ethan before he even starts," Mom says, as she tosses the pasta box in a recycling bin. Without stopping she moves to the overhead cabinets that hold her hand-made plates and bowls. "And maybe Spooner will get his act together."

We finish setting salad plates, forks, knives, and spoons on the table just as my dad pushes through the back porch door into the kitchen. When he leaves work as a software developer, Dad takes the Seattle-Soltrice ferry right after Mom's commute. We usually eat as soon as he arrives.

Mom shoots Dad a quick smile and Justin pumps the spinner, suddenly very serious about his job.

Setting his laptop case down on a beat-up, red wicker chair by the door, Dad beams as he watches Mom dish up mounds of spaghetti in four large bowls for us to carry to the table. *Can they move any faster? I'm really hungry.*

Both of my parents are smart, in their own ways. Not me. My second grade teacher, Miss Mills, described me as "average" and "has trouble remembering words." I'd seen those comments on a report she sent to my parents. She'd also written the words "tries very hard." I didn't like the idea that I was just "average."

"Hi boys. Anyone been good today?" That's Dad's standard greeting to us, which he delivers smiling over Mom's shoulder as he hugs her.

Justin and I sit down at the table with our bowls of spaghetti. Dad pours glasses of wine for Mom and himself.

"Anything new with you?" he asks me, as he adds more dressing to his salad. Justin twirls a massive loop of noodles around his fork. He can't get the full glob in his mouth, and half the noodles slide back to his plate.

"Yeah. Spooner got cut for drugs."

"Hmm. What drugs?"

"Coach didn't say."

"And you don't know?"

I ignore the question.

"Do you think the school will let him play soccer this spring?" Dad asks, pointing to a dish of grated cheese and gesturing meaningfully at Justin.

"Doubtful. Coach Davis already gave him a second chance last year. I guess Coach will move someone up." I try not to think about whether Spooner's not playing spring soccer will mean I'll have to rotate to yet another position.

"Well, too bad," Dad says slowly, holding my eyes for a few seconds like he always does when he wants me to continue. "Seems like there's more to that story," he says, and waits. I shrug, and act like I haven't heard him. Actually, I don't want to talk with my parents about the drugs I know Spooner has been doing because it's Spooner's problem, not mine.

Dad frowns slightly before turning to Justin. "What about you, my friend? What happened in your world today?"

Justin launches into something about sliding tectonic plates that he'd learned in his sixth-grade science class. My thoughts return to Mackie. *How can I arrange to be with her again at the shelter? Maybe I should speak with Olivia, our volunteer coordinator, and see if she will schedule us together? She'll think I'm crushing on Mackie, which is close to the truth. That and I really want to figure out what's up with Mackie and the animals' unusual behavior.*

After we finish dinner, I help clear the dishes. Mom stands at the sink, washing the pasta pot. "Jeremy, you remember that tomorrow night Dad and I will be in Seattle. Right?" she asks.

"Sure. You have some stuff in a show."

"Yes, and Justin is going to a sleepover."

My phone buzzes. It's Olivia, at the wildlife shelter:

Jeremy can U work Friday nite 6-10? Sorry 4 the late Q.

I turn my screen to show Mom the message. She nods.

The wildlife shelter operates on four-hour volunteer shifts around the clock. Olivia won't be there, so I can't ask her about working with Mackie. That will have to wait until next week. Frowning, I send an immediate reply, "Yes."

Chapter 2

I wake to buzzing in my ear. Searching around for my alarm I want, for maybe the bazillionth time, another hour of sleep. But to catch a ride to school with Ben, I need to move.

Looking in the bathroom mirror, I turn on the cold water, splash some on my face, and swipe deodorant on my 'pits. Life doesn't suck, but nothing really exciting is happening either, except what I've seen going down at the shelter. I dry my face in a hand towel, and peer closer in the mirror for traces of a beard. *Still nothing.*

Dressed and moving downstairs, I head for the kitchen. Mom doesn't teach an early class today. She's set up a breakfast of cereal and fruit, and keeps an eye on the clock for Justin and me. After I rinse my bowl and set it in the dishwasher, she follows me through the hallway and vestibule to the outside door.

Smiling back at her, I try to register her last words as I exit down our front porch steps. "You have burritos in the freezer for dinner. Make yourself a salad, please, and don't be out too late. Dad and I will be back on the ten-thirty ferry. Remember to set your alarm for tomorrow. Okay?"

"Okay. Thanks," I mumble, waving a hand over my shoulder. Ben watches my slug-like pace toward his car. The morning air feels comfortably cool and the saltwater smell from Puget Sound drifts in on a breeze. It's a fine September day.

"Hey," I say, as I adjust my backpack and fasten the seat belt.

"'Morning," he returns.

It's our usual quiet ride to school, but I don't mind. Being with Ben's a lot easier than being with some of the more social guys. He stays within himself, but it's not like he's unfriendly. Ben just thinks more than most of us.

Guiding his grandpa's old Honda into an assigned parking space not far from the west side of school, Ben rouses himself. "You need a ride in tomorrow?"

"That'd be great. Don't you wish this was a home meet?"

"Yeah. I'll be by at a quarter of six." Ben kills the engine, and opens his door.

"Thanks," I say as I heave myself out of the car. Ben peels off toward B Building, and I walk through the parking lot looking around for anyone I know. *Will I get to see Mackie before class starts?*

Standing near the crowded Student Lounge in C Building, I rub my eyes, trying to wake up as trumpeting voices bounce off the pale-yellow masonry walls. The usual cliques have assembled in the hallway—the jocks, the jocks' girlfriends, the techies, the druggies, various geek groups, and the wannabes. I pass the Jesus Freaks. I don't buy what they're selling. My motto is "see and verify."

"Jeremy."

I turn to find Erica, Jon, and Wendy. The four of us are part of a larger group of friends who've known each other since kindergarten. We eat lunch together at school and hang out on weekends. Wendy links her arm in mine and pulls me forward. We begin to walk.

"Are you ready for the quiz?" she asks.

"No. There's a quiz today? You're playing me."

"Like you didn't study. Miss a question. C'mon." She nods her head to get me to agree.

I grin as we march up the stairway. Wendy and I have been friendly rivals since third grade. She's like a girl-version of myself: someone who wants to know how, and why, things work. A while back, I was crushing on her, but she acted like a good friend and no more, so that went nowhere. Anyway, she knows that I read our U.S. History assignments. Even though it does take me forever.

After I finish the quiz, I open my notebook and pretend to study our next history assignment. I'll see Mackie at lunch and might be able to find out when she's scheduled to work again at the shelter. I can't be too pushy, though, or she'll wonder why I ask. Still, it would be great if she were also interested in me. Yeah, that would be cool, for her to look into my eyes, lean forward . . .

At the end of class, Wendy and I find out that we've tied at 95%. We both fell for the same trick question. Mr. Wakely, beaming proudly, explains the reason why there can be only one correct answer to his true or false question: "Supply was the deciding factor in the North's victory over the South." It turns out that "supply *and finance*" were deciding factors.

As we leave class, Wendy calls out, "Jeremy, next time. Next time you're going down."

She flips her long hair around like a martial arts weapon and grins. I shake my head, pretending not to know what she means. We both smile.

I weave through student-clogged hallways to Computer Lab and sit down. As I pull out my notebook, Brody walks in and comes straight at me. He looks pissed. The small of my back pushes against my chair, and my feet press down hard on the floor, my skin suddenly hot.

Brody glares at the guy in the cubicle next to mine. The kid grabs his books and moves away without saying a word. Brody leans against the edge of the now-vacant desk.

"What's up?" I ask, not really wanting to know.

"Why didn't you say that you and Mackie were together all the time? At the animal shelter."

"Didn't think it mattered."

"Hey, I asked you if you knew what was going on with her, if she was seeing anyone, and you didn't tell me about that."

I stare at him. What does he want?

"Anything else you forgot to tell me?" he asks.

"Nothing to tell. We both volunteer at the shelter. So?"

"You better not be messing with me." He touches his right index finger to his head and taps. Like always, Brody just has to show that he's in control.

Then, he leans over and jabs the same finger into my chest.

I rise out of my seat, squaring my shoulders, ready for anything. Mrs. Leonard, the Computer Lab monitor, walks up, frowning. "No talking. Let's try and use our time wisely, please."

Brody stretches a "good-boy" smile at her. She smiles back at him and then shakes her head at me. *How am I the bad guy?*

After Computer Lab, Brody gives me a hard look, but doesn't say anything. I want to punch him. A voice in my head says, *leave it.* I need to eat lunch.

Everyone is seated at our table when I enter the packed Dining Hall. Wendy motions that she will make space for me. Guess she isn't too upset about our 95% tie.

Mackie sits directly across from me at the table, talking with Erica. I give her a friendly nod. I really want to sit next to her. She sends a quick grin back and waves to Wendy. Suddenly, as if she can hear my thoughts, Mackie looks back at me with a big smile. *Too weird.*

I glance to my right. A few tables down, Brody sits with his arm around Jilly, apparently unconcerned that Mackie is so near, and that I'm sitting across from her. Brody. The guy is one big contradiction. Or maybe the game rules have shifted.

After lunch, I walk out next to Mackie. My curiosity about when she will work again at the wildlife shelter is greater than my recent shyness around her. "Hey, Mackie. Are you working at the shelter today?" I manage to sound reasonably casual, though I hear my heartbeat echo like a roll of thunder.

She turns her eyes that can charm an eagle into submission up at me. "Olivia reworked my schedule. I'm on the evening shift," she says in a surprised tone.

I can't believe my ears. *Together! Tonight!* I control an urge to leap in the air and smack the ceiling light, or, worse, grab her arms and swing her around like a little girl. Instead, I manage to stay cool.

"Are you working, too?" she asks.

"Uh, yeah. I didn't know Olivia was making adjustments. It's good; good that we're working tonight. Together." I bite my lower lip. *That sounded really lame.* We head into our English Literature class, where I spend most of the session trying to pay attention as Mrs. Littlejohn expounds on the "still relevant" themes of Charles Dickens. Following alphabetic seating rules, Mackie sits in front of me. I'm happy that our last names beginning "S" and "T" have me sitting behind her.

After sixth period, cross-country has a pre-race meeting. Coach motions for us to follow him, and we sit outside on the track's sun-warmed, metal bleachers.

"Tonight, get some sleep. Tomorrow morning, six o'clock sharp, we're leaving from the front parking lot for the ferry. I want everyone suited up, ready to run. Don't forget your shoes." He looks pointedly at Trace Benton, and a couple of the guys laugh.

Coach passes out copies of the course map. "Bring money or a ticket for the ferry. Also, very important, Ethan will run as our varsity alternate. His times are good enough to move him up. Tomorrow, we go out as a team and Ethan's part of our team. Okay, remember your strategies, what we talked about this week. Think about how you're going to run the course. Get in your zone. And be here on time. That's it." He whacks his clipboard against the bleacher to signal that we're done.

I settle in for another quiet ride home with Ben. We weave through residential streets lined with tall, thick Douglas firs and mature cedars. In my neighborhood, homes are set so far back you see only the openings of driveways. We're within a quarter mile of Puget Sound and the air smells of saltwater and woodsy, organic decay. For me, that has always been the familiar scent of home.

Ben pulls into our laurel-lined circle drive and stops at the halfway point.

"See you. Early," he says.

"Yeah, too early," I reply, climbing out of my seat.

Ben snorts his agreement. He gears the Honda into first, and eases around the other side of the drive back to the road.

As Ben leaves, I stand at the base of our porch stairs, searching the bottom of my gear bag for keys to the front door. I like being the first one home after school. I have all the space to myself. Not a grand place like some on the island, our house has been my home since I was born. I remember the day my dad told me it was built in the 1940s to resemble a small country lodge, with a river-rock base. Blue-gray rocks merge with cedar siding, topped by a dark green metal roof.

I open the outer door and pick out a second key for entrance from the vestibule to the foyer. Because my dad designs security software and keeps files at home, we observe a number of protocols. Cameras are stationed at all outer doorways. I like to sometimes make faces at those, and one time got Justin to put on a gorilla mask so I could lift him right up to a lens. After the police came out on a silent run, I had to explain to them, and Dad, about the mask. We decided fooling with the system wasn't such a good idea. I saw a smile on Dad's face though, when he reviewed the security shots.

In our family room, a river-rock half-wall sits behind a red wood stove, used when temperatures drop below freezing. Worn, wicker chairs and a big couch top a thick braided rug. Mom's clay, raku, and stoneware pots are everywhere. Dad calls it Lodge-Chic. Mom wrinkles her nose at him when he says that. I like the place just fine, especially the woodsy smell from the overhead cedar beams.

I flop down on the couch for a quick nap. Later, treading in my socks down the creaky, wood-floored hallway to the kitchen,

I wonder who will be on rotation at the shelter. Three volunteers always work one shift. *An adult will be with us, but who?*

I could text Mackie to ask if she wants to walk to the shelter together. That might come off as too pushy. Her family lives nearby in a waterfront home that overlooks the Puget Sound to Seattle. They have views of the city, the water, and the Cascade Mountains.

Remembering Mom's dinner instructions, I microwave and slam down two burritos, then eat a mashed up fistful of leaf lettuce. I examine my teeth in the glass door of a kitchen cabinet, and gulp some water to rinse my mouth, but decide not to chance a hanging green erratic. I sprint upstairs, brush my teeth, and pull an old fleece-lined jacket from my closet.

Skipping down the stairs, I snatch my set of keys from the kitchen peg, and flip my phone, flashlight, and bike reflector into a small gear bag. Finally, I put on a pair of old training shoes, and take off at a trot.

The western sun feels like a spray of heat on my face. Keeping to the soft road shoulder, I breathe in a mixed scent of sweet cedar needles and leaves. Yeah, late summer is my favorite time of the year. I need to store this up for January and February. That's when the Northwest becomes dense green with gray-grim skies.

I find the white entrance post to the shelter. The Olympic Wildlife Shelter is partially hidden behind a stand of tall Douglas firs. The one-level, ranch-style building holds an administrative office and rooms for animal recovery. To the south of the building, open-air cages let animals in advanced recovery stages build and test their strength before release back into the wild.

I enter through the main door, see Mrs. Walton, and smile. She's our adult volunteer for the shift. An ex-Navy nurse, Mrs. Walton is also a grandma, and someone I've always liked being around.

She looks up brightly at me. "Hello, Jeremy. Looks like it's you, Mackenzie Spence, and me tonight. I've been working mornings, so I haven't met the Spence girl."

"She just started this summer. We're friends."

"Good. We should be able to easily handle what's here. Most of the critters only need feeding and cleanup."

As she speaks, I reach into a locker and pull out a men's large, olive drab work coverall. Stepping in and zipping the coverall over my clothes, I hear the door open. *Mackie.*

Her long hair is pulled up in a braid that begins at the top of her head and trails down her back. She pauses just inside the doorway, slightly flushed. Maybe she ran, too?

"Hey, Jer," she says, removing her sunglasses and tucking them in her shirt pocket. Then she notices Mrs. Walton and goes to her with a hand extended, speaking in an out-of-breath voice, "Hi, I'm Mackie Spence."

Mrs. Walton checks her out, shakes Mackie's hand, and says, "Winifred Walton. We're the team tonight so let's get to it. We'll look in on surgery patients first, then do feeding and cleaning. It's the usual drill."

I nod as I lock the front door. The shelter is now closed for the evening.

Mackie has climbed into her coveralls. The three of us move quietly into the Recovery Hall, the smell of disinfectant and animal urine in a seventy-two-degree building hitting me in a wave. Like always, I flinch from that particular combination of odors and heat.

"Two of my grandchildren are coming to visit me tomorrow morning so I'd like to leave early tonight if at all possible," Mrs. Walton says.

We put on hoods, masks, and gloves that protect recovering wildlife from identifying humans as non-threatening. We want to look like aliens, something the animals will never see again.

"Okay," Mrs. Walton says as we pause outside the first doorway off the Recovery Hall. She reads from a clipboard that contains medical notes from Doc Kemp, our on-call veterinarian. "Hmm . . . we have a young fawn. A car hit her. Looks like she has a fractured front leg, set yesterday, and some nasty road-rash cuts."

Mrs. Walton opens the door, and we enter the room without speaking. The fawn lies on her side and blinks rapidly as we approach. Restraints, along with sedatives, have otherwise immobilized her.

Mrs. Walton motions for Mackie and me to wait near the door. There is no sense in upsetting the young deer with all of us getting close. Then Mrs. Walton moves in to look at the wounds. The fawn turns her eyes to Mackie. I notice that the deer relaxes. Relaxing isn't normal for a wild animal with humans so near. Mackie begins to tremble slightly. That's something I've seen her do before, when she and animals new to the shelter first look at each other.

Mrs. Walton carefully examines the restraint harness around the fawn to make sure it is intact before lifting loose bandages from cut areas. Applying salve through a small caulking gun, she doesn't touch the deer with her hands. At the shelter, we try to keep all of our actions slow and clean. Mrs. Walton is a nursing pro, and the fawn stays calm, only moving as the salve is spread. Within a few minutes the sutures are dressed and Mrs. Walton inserts another bottle of intravenous fluid into the holder.

Back in the hallway, Mrs. Walton nods. "She's already healing. I like her prognosis."

Next, we enter a room that houses several injured raccoons. Most have been hurt by traps, but one juvenile has escaped a coyote attack, losing its tail and an ear. Again, the same protocols are observed and again, the animals noticeably relax after making eye contact with Mackie. Since Mackie doesn't tremble, I figure that she's maybe met the raccoons during some earlier volunteer session.

Proceeding to two more quiet rooms, we look in on a couple of injured ducks, a goose, and an opossum. Again, the animals stay calm and show Mackie respect. Mrs. Walton seems unaware of anything out of the ordinary. *Am I the only one who notices how the animals respond to Mackie?*

Now finished with the severe trauma cases, we retrace our steps through the hall to gather food and water. Pushing through the swing doors into the main room, Mrs. Walton looks pleased.

"That's what I like to see: stable and improving animals," she says.

"It seems like we have more raccoons lately," I say.

"Yes," Mrs. Walton replies. "Usually that happens earlier in the summer, after the kits are born and moving around."

"I saw you give one of the juvenile raccoons another injection. Isn't he healing?" Mackie asks, her voice soft.

"He had surgery yesterday and seemed too alert today, so I gave him more to sleep. An incarcerated, unhappy raccoon could tear the hell out of this place and take us on, too. Why don't you both feed the birds and I'll look in on the coyote pup that's in the small pen."

"Okay," I say happily. Mackie nods. Of course I'm pleased to be alone with her. We head for the feed bins, just off the main room.

"I'll get the water," I say. While I hoist a five-gallon container of water on my shoulder, she scoops seed and grubs into bowls. We walk down the linoleum-lined hallway that leads to the back door.

As we exit the building, we can still see without additional light. The birds are caged outside, in a Small Flight Cage rehab box. Near the Large Flight Cage, the small box is used as a first step for birds that still need to regain their strength.

As we approach, the sound of our feet crunching down on the tree bark-lined trail alerts three American crows. The *Corvus brachyrhynchos* straighten to attention. I mouth the words to myself, trying hard to remember the Latin genus and species pronunciation. They dip their heads slightly and appear to bow. In my years of volunteering at the shelter, that behavior has never been directed at humans. I suspect it's because of Mackie's presence.

Resisting the urge to ask Mackie about it, I struggle to keep the shelter protocols for silence. I rinse and restock the ground-level birdbath while she empties the seed tray. Then, Mackie splashes some water inside to clean the shallow dish and dries it with a paper towel. Finally, she adds the seed and fruit. Moving on to the grub bowl, which has been picked clean, Mackie scoops in fat, wriggling grubs. *Yum!* Then we retreat and close the gate.

We've saved the best for last: Diana, our resident Barred Owl. *Strix varia*. She came to the shelter during its first year of operation and has been a star teaching assistant ever since. With a damaged right wing, Diana can't fly, but she accompanies our wildlife director on field trips to schools and speaking events. My favorite at the shelter, Diana has spooky, glass-brown eyes and dark, striped markings running vertically on her chest feathers. Her call pattern to other owls in the surrounding woods is a cadence of eight hoots, in groups of four.

I have a gutted, defrosted mouse for her, a top pick on any owl's menu. As we approach, Diana gives a low *hoo-hoo*. She knows her dinnertime, and it makes me happy to see her reaction to the food. Tonight, however, she doesn't put on a show of lifting her wings to remind me of her superior size. After Mackie appears, Diana becomes quiet and lowers her eyes.

I leave the mouse near her on a feeding dish and clean up the smelly owl pellets under her perch. If they aren't removed daily, oh *gach*! The stench can get bad fast. I scoop and bag the waste, and Mackie and I exit through the door.

Once inside the main building again, I struggle to frame my 'Big Question.' Removing my mask, I say, "Ah, Mackie, you seem to have an odd effect on animals."

She doesn't respond and continues to walk toward the food bins. I easily match her pace, knowing she's heard the question in my comment.

"It's not a criticism. I just want to understand, because I've never seen anything like it before."

Mackie dumps the unused seed from her pail into the bin and ignores me.

"Hey look, I'm just trying to figure out why you get a special response from the animals."

She takes off her goggles and hood, and shakes her braid loose. "Do you need to know why? Does everything have to have an explanation?"

"Well, yeah. I've been volunteering here for almost two years and no one gets the kind of reactions you get. Why?"

"Why do the animals react, or why have you never seen the same reactions?"

At least she's replied. Then she turns her dark eyes with their thickly fringed, black lashes to meet mine, and I falter, nearly losing my stream of thought. Silence.

"Uh, okay, I'll give you an example. Remember when you first started volunteering here? Number 26, the bald eagle that right away deferred to you? That's not normal behavior. She gave you respect. And just now, in all the rooms, the animals relaxed when you walked in. That's not normal. So how do you explain it?" I stop talking when I see her frown. Then her eyes soften and I plunge in again.

"I'm not saying that you're not normal. But the animals all seem to have reactions to you that they don't have around other people."

She smiles her sad smile and shrugs her shoulders. "Jeremy, after we graduate are you going to study wildlife biology at the U?"

"I've thought about it. Why aren't you answering my questions?"

"What if I don't have answers to your questions?" she responds, holding my eyes in hers with a steady look that silently advises me to drop it.

In all our years of growing up together she's never been evasive with me. Why now?

Then the doors swing open. Mrs. Walton marches in with a clipboard, announcing happily, "Okay. We're buttoned down for the evening." She looks at her watch. "It's nine hundred fifteen hours. I really need to get home. I'm going to trust the two of you to finish up."

"Sounds good," I say quickly. "We'll do a load of laundry until the next shift gets here."

Mackie nods.

With that, Mrs. Walton picks up her tote and says goodbye. We hear her old car moan and chug unsteadily as she pulls up the hill to the road.

I look back at Mackie, and we walk toward the laundry room.

"Mackie, we've known each other since we were kids. What's different now?" I push, hoping to appeal to our friendship.

"I really don't know what to say about the animals. Maybe they like my scent."

I raise my eyebrows at her.

"Really, I mean it. Couldn't what you're seeing be their reaction to my body chemistry or something? Does it have to be something bigger?"

Her attempt to disarm me isn't going to work. I know too much about the animal kingdom. I shift from one foot to the other, trying to come up with a fresh tactic to get her to open up.

"Yeah, well, I can see how an animal would find you attractive," I say clumsily and hasten to add, "But that's because you're so cute."

She sticks her tongue out at me.

"What I don't get is why the animals show you respect."

"Respect," she repeats, cocking her head like the concept has never occurred to her.

"Come on Mackie." Now it's Mackie who searches my eyes for an answer. I sense I have the advantage and press on. "You know what's going on is out of the ordinary. What is it?"

She takes my right hand in hers and says, "Jeremy, am I so unexciting that it takes animals reacting to me in odd ways to get your attention?" I feel really thrown off my game.

I became the silent one. Did she just flirt with me? No. Everything about her seems serious.

We hear a muffled cry. Mackie drops my hand.

Reaching quickly for my hood and goggles, I say, "Probably one of the raccoons."

My soft-soled shoes make light, *thip-thip* sounds as I run through the hallway to the raccoons' room at the far end of the corridor. But the room is still, the animals curled into sleep balls. *What was that sound?* I hurry, looking in the windowed doors of the rooms along the hallway. Now it is ominously quiet. Where did the noise come from?

Leaving the Recovery Hall at a trot, I run through the main room and into the laundry room. Mackie isn't there. I run to the back door leading to the flight cages and step outside.

Twilight has made the transition to darkness. My eyes strain to adjust as the cooling night air hits my face. Where is Mackie?

Hearing a sound to my left, I wheel. Someone is in the cage with Number 26. Moving toward the figure, I pick out a familiar, wheedling voice.

"Here, little birdie, come to papa. Come to the feedbag, birdie. Where are you? You freaking bird. Yeah, you're coming with me."

It's Brody. That bone head! He must be on something, thinking he can just walk in and take an eagle out with him. Then I stop. Someone else is in the cage with him. *Mackie?*

"Brody, don't move," she says in a commanding voice. "Don't move an inch."

For a moment it's quiet. Then I hear the slight whooshing sound of Number 26 as she flies through the upper reaches of the cage. I want to move, but my feet stay rooted to the ground.

Not Mackie, no, whispers a voice inside my head.

Mackie has moved between Brody and Number 26, her back turned to Brody. She lifts her arms in a T-shape in front of him as the eagle gathers speed. It's all playing out like a bad horror film. The eagle dives in attack. Mackie stands in the way.

But suddenly, Number 26 struggles out of her assault and alights on an upper perch. She screams in alarm, dropping her head and retracting her wings. Number 26 isn't attacking anymore. She's demonstrating submission!

"Brody, move. Get out." Mackie speaks in a low, but forceful voice.

Brody doesn't move, so she switches to a sweet voice, "That's right. Back to the gate." She shoves him through the opening, and I feel myself breathe again.

I want to tackle Brody. Hard. Mackie could have been hurt. Number 26 might be re-injured. As I come at them in a sprint, Mackie holds up a hand and shakes her head for me to stop. Rocking back on my heels, I manage to halt. Just barely.

"Let's get him inside," she whispers, her voice shaking with urgency.

Brody has gone quiet, though I don't trust him to behave. Mackie takes the lead followed by Brody, who stumbles like he could fall over. I trail both as we return to the shelter's main building.

Once inside, I grab Brody by the front of his shirt. "What were you thinking?"

He looks at me like I'm the crazy one. "Jer, you need to get a life. Hanging out here with Mackie? What's up with that?"

I bite my lower lip.

"Just wanted to see how big she was." Brody makes a flapping motion with his arms like a bird in flight, spirals in a circle, and collapses on the floor.

Keeping her eyes on Brody, Mackie edges over to the window.

"I don't see his car. How did he get here?" she asks.

I walk to her and squint at the parking lot. "Right. I don't see it either. I'll call and see if Jake can pick him up." I reach inside my coveralls for my cell phone and dial for information. Brody's older brother Jake lives at home for his freshman year at the U. Unlike Brody, Jake has always been a straight-up guy.

Jake answers my call.

"Hey, it's Jeremy Tarleton. Your brother's passed out at the wildlife shelter. Are you picking him up, or should I feed him to the coyotes?" I ask in a tight voice.

"Tempting, but I'll come get him," Jake answers.

"Dim your lights when you pull in, okay?"

Mackie and I stand in front of Brody. We each take one of his hands in our own and drag him outside onto the front entrance stoop. Mackie says she wants to check on Number 26. I don't ask if she needs help. Clearly, she and the eagle are on very good terms with one another.

I stand guard over Brody, who remains out of it. When Mackie returns she says, "Number 26 seems to be okay. I let her know things will be fine."

I let her know things will be fine? How could she let Number 26 know something like that? This is one of several questions I have for Mackenzie Allison Spence, including why didn't Number 26 complete her attack? But first I want Brody gone, before the next shift of volunteers arrives.

Within a few minutes we hear a car nearing. Jake has turned his headlights down to dim. He pulls up near the front entrance and exits the car, not bothering to close the front door.

"Damn. Did he hurt anyone?" Jake asks, walking to us and shaking his head when he notices his brother.

"No. I'll help you get him in the car," I offer.

Jake grimaces, nods to Mackie, and eyes Brody like he doesn't particularly want to claim him. Shaking his head, he turns to me. "Get the back door, okay?"

Walking to the car, I say, "I don't know what his deal is, but he tried to mess with an eagle that could have shredded him."

"He's lucky," Jake replies.

Then Jake, a former 170-pound high school wrestler, half-carries, half-shoves his brother to the car. We lay him on the back seat. Brody's still totally out of it.

Jake frowns, again, as he climbs into the driver's seat.

"Thanks," he says. "He probably won't even remember this." Jake turns back for a quick look at his younger brother before starting the car. Then they leave.

Mackie sits on a bench near the front door, her shoulders slumped forward.

"Mackie, you okay?" I ask.

"Maybe I'll get some water," she says, standing. We re-enter the building. "Should we report this?"

"If we do, they'll never let anyone our age work alone again," I answer.

She shoots me a question with her eyes.

"What's Brody going to do? File a complaint against us for interrupting his trying to steal an eagle? Anyway, how did he get in the cage?" I ask.

"I don't know. He was already inside when I saw him."

"It should have been locked," I mutter.

Mackie fills a cup at the water dispenser. Her face has become pale, and she trembles. This maybe isn't a good time to ask her more questions. Still, after what I saw and heard tonight, I know she can come up with better answers.

We finish putting the day's used towels and linens in the washer, and are making some final notes on the daily Report Sheet when the next shift arrives.

Mackie and I toss our hoods into the laundry basket and return our coveralls to the hanging pegs. After putting our goggles and gloves away, we walk out the front door. It closes behind us, with a self-locking click.

Pausing outside, Mackie touches my arm. "Jeremy, could I ask you something?"

"I have a flashlight and reflector to loan you . . ." She smiles down at the ground like there's some inside joke.

Then she looks back up, more serious, and asks, "Would you walk me home?"

Chapter 3

That irritating sound, the buzz of my alarm clock next to my ear! Groaning, I reach for the off button. I was having the best dream ever, and want to stay in bed.

Then I sit up, fast. It wasn't a dream, or a fantasy. It actually happened. Yesterday. But, Ben will be in our driveway any minute. We have a cross-country race to run this morning.

I dash into the bathroom between Justin's and my room. It's early, so brotherly competition for the facilities isn't a problem. I slap cold water on my face and put on my tank, shorts, and school warmups. Picking up my gear bag, I smile, thinking about what happened the night before, after Mackie and I left the shelter. It began when she asked me to walk her home.

"Sure," I said. Then I noticed she was shivering. "Mackie, here, put this on. Really, I don't need it."

She slipped into my jacket and zipped it up. Mackie's over a half-foot shorter than me, and my jacket hung almost to her knees. Then she reached over and put her left arm behind my back at my waist, resting her hand on my hip like it was something she did every day.

To steady myself, I put my hand around her right shoulder. At that moment, I couldn't think of any questions to ask her. I was speechless as we moved away from the building, walking in step with each other. *My arm was around Mackie!* She'd been my friend for years. But now she was grown-up Mackie, who spun my head around every time she walked near me.

I handed her my flashlight and pulled out my reflector to give us more visibility, since it was a star-masked night.

"What did Brody mean when he asked about your hanging out with me?" she asked.

"Who knows?"

"Why do you think he went after Number 26?"

"He's Mr. Adventure. Didn't he mention that when you guys were together?"

"Brody has a lot of problems," she said.

"Like more than drinking too much?" I asked.

"Yeah."

"Did he ever do anything around you?"

"He asked me if I wanted to try something once. I didn't."

We fell silent. Brody was trouble. But with Mackie next to me I didn't want to talk about him. Her hair smelled like vanilla and oranges and her body warmth felt fantastic against me.

When we arrived at her house, she turned toward me. "Will you wait while I tell Mom and Dad I'm home? We could sit on the porch for awhile."

Still stunned from the walk, I nodded obediently, like a third grader. I had a new numb feeling: a vacant spot where my brain seemed to have left my head.

Mackie returned, handed me my jacket, and wrapped a red fleece blanket around herself. She motioned for me to sit next to her on the porch swing.

I'd been on that porch hundreds of times since I was a kid, but never had my heart hammered so hard. Mackie took my hand in hers. Then she moved closer to me, so that her head rested on my shoulder. I reached up and brought my arm behind her neck, pulling her hair braid over her shoulder. Then I cupped the loose, silky ends of her hair.

I could not breathe.

"Jeremy, have you read the story of the man who wakes up in bed and believes he's become an insect?" Mackie asked.

"Kafka. *The Metamorphosis*."

"Is it real or is it a dream? Or maybe it's an explanation of how life is lived," she said.

Mackie paused. "I'm telling you this because you have questions. But I'm still trying to figure things out myself."

I nodded, wanting her to explain more.

"After the accident this summer, I've felt different. What's important to me has changed so much that most of our friends would be surprised. I don't think you would, though." She stopped and our eyes locked.

As if some invisible force guided us, we moved our heads closer. We kissed! I'd kissed three other girls in my life, once on a dare when I was thirteen, then there was my ninth-grade crush Robin Pembroke, and last year a couple of times with Cat Morley.

But this was different! It was a really sweet kiss, like we were taking each other's lips' taste and temperature. Her lips felt warm and soft; their taste, a little salty. As the kiss lengthened, I felt an electric shock run through my body. Finally, I adjusted my arm because it started to ache. I moved so that I could sit closer to her and our second kiss lit me up inside. I could have spent the rest of the night exploring her lips.

Hearing a noise at the front door, we quickly parted. Mackie's dad, Nick Spence, stepped out on the porch and asked if we wanted to come in for popcorn and a late movie.

I heard Mackie sigh. "No thanks, Dad. It's a nice night to sit outside."

"Okay, but it's a thriller."

After Mr. Spence left, Mackie laid her head on my shoulder again. "I've wondered what kind of a kisser you were. Definitely worth the wait. Who knew you'd be so hot after all these years," she added, grinning.

"You think I'm hot?"

"Yeah. You don't know how many girls are crushing on you."

She said it very matter-of-factly, but it was hard for me to believe. I've never seen myself that way. I was the "average" kid.

I laughed a little. "I think you're talking about the wrong person. Do you know how many guys practically self-combust when you're around?"

She smiled and shifted to look at me. "I hope we can see more of each other," she said.

"Yeah, I'd really like that. I mean, I like being with you."

Mackie grinned.

Uh-oh. Saying more could get me in trouble. I was suddenly aware of the time. "Hey, Ben's picking me up at a quarter of six tomorrow. Maybe I can call you in the afternoon?" She looked pleased. "After I get back?"

"Cool," she said.

I jogged home, with my flashlight bobbing and my head spinning. A soft breeze tickled at my nose. Who knew it was possible to feel so happy? Even my feet felt lighter. And I managed to return home before my parents. *Outstanding!*

• • •

I stand in the cool morning air on our front porch, my mushy memories interrupted all-too-soon by the sound of Ben's Honda crunching down our gravel drive. He looks tired, and I probably look far worse. I had six and a half hours of sleep last night, more like five factoring in the time I spent in bed trying to calm down after returning home.

Ben pulls into the school's courtesy lot, next to our teammates whose cars are parked in a tight pack by the main entrance. We haul our gear bags from the back seat. The guys bounce on their feet to keep warm as they huddle around Coach. Everyone's together, except for Cole Pinchot and Brody. Cole is a senior, our Number

Two runner, and a real morning person. He stands close to Brody, jabbering. Brody looks ready to smack him.

Brody. I will probably have to deal with him about what happened last night with Number 26. To my relief, he doesn't even look in my direction. Could Jake be right, and Brody doesn't remember being at the shelter?

"Okay," Coach is wide-awake and in charge. "These kind ladies," he beams at the moms and Mrs. Showalter, a history teacher, "are your chauffeurs today. When you're in their cars, I expect you to behave like the gentlemen I know you can be. No cussing, no fighting, and no sass. It's a beautiful day for a morning run. Pick up your gear. Find a car. Let's move."

I like Coach's attitude about racing: "A beautiful day for a morning run." If he only knew what makes it so exceptional for me. I still feel stoked from being with Mackie.

I climb in Mrs. Showalter's car with Ben and Ryan Long. Ryan's our elite runner who finished second at State last year as a junior. He runs a 15:40.00 5K. Today, we hope he will be number one in the individual competition, and put us over the top for the meet overall. Ryan pops in his earbuds. He has his tunes and race plan prepped. It will be a quiet ride.

Mrs. Showalter greets us. "Good morning. You have splendid weather today. I heard on the radio that it's fifty-three degrees and dry in Seattle. And the pollution index is very good. Okay, does everyone have his seat belt on?" In a few minutes Mrs. Showalter eases down the road, and we pay at the ferry ticket gate. Then we line up for the six-thirty boat.

Once we're on the ferry, everyone seems to relax. Ben rests his head back against the seat. Rumbling sleep sounds escape from his mouth. As she opens her door, Mrs. Showalter turns back in and asks if we want anything from the galley. I shake my head no. Ryan nods his head to his music, oblivious to the question. After

Mrs. Showalter leaves, I close my eyes to better picture my running inspiration: *Mackie.*

. . .

We roll into Seattle's Riley City Park. Coach has arranged for us to meet in a parking lot near the course, and everyone congregates around him.

"Hey, listen up," Coach yells. Fifteen excited voices get quiet in a hurry.

"We have fifty minutes before the start. Three things I want from you before this race: First, leave your gear with your drivers. As you can see, the ladies are setting their chairs up near the start. Second, check in at the registration table and get your numbers. Now, very important, put your number cards on the front and back of your tank immediately. Third, I want all of you to walk or jog this course. I know, some of you ran it last year, but check it out again. Take your maps and follow the flags. There may be some changes.

"One more thing: Pay attention to the time. I'll be very disappointed if I see anyone still on the course or running out of the Port-a-Potty when the start horn sounds.

"After the race, pick up your gear bags. We'll take the ten-forty boat home, leaving this parking lot at ten o'clock. Anyone not in a car will be left behind. We're not waiting around. Is that clear? Good. Ribbons will be sent to me at school. Any questions? Now, I know every one of you guys can better your times today. Remember your race strategy and stick to it. We went over that last week. Right? Okay, have a good race. Let's get it!"

Coach claps his hands. An East-coast runner in his college days, his eyes are fired up. For an old guy, he still feels race day.

With arm-pumping and hand-clapping, we follow our pre-competition routine. Just the way it does before every race, my stomach turns cold and jittery. To warm up and stay loose, I make myself jog and try to memorize the race flags on the course. The damp air feels cool in contrast to the heat under my skin. Anything is possible. Completing my practice loop, I have one thought: *I am going to kill this course!*

Five minutes before the start, Ryan pulls his earbuds and drops his music in his gear bag. He looks detached, his race face. With my teammates, I maneuver into a swarm of thirty-five varsity runners as we position ourselves within the wide start box. I suck in a big breath and let it out when the horn sounds. I'm running the first straightaway. This race is mine to win!

• • •

I cross the finish line in what seems like slow motion, pushing against the air. Heat sears my lungs and muscle contractions shoot through my legs. Ugh! My legs. They're like two burning sticks of lactic acid. I know that I've run a much-better-than-average time. At just over seventeen minutes, it's a full thirty seconds lower than my former best. Panting, I coast over to Ryan, who breathes hard but somehow still manages to move fluidly.

"How'd you do?" I gasp. He puts up an index finger. Ryan brought us a first place finish! That will be really great for our standing in the team tally. And of course, he's pulled out a big individual win for himself, too.

"You?" he asks.

Grinning from pain and happiness, I gasp out my time, "17:10.02." Ryan whistles and raises his fist for a bump. He knows what shaving thirty seconds off my best time means to me, and to the team.

As I search for our jersey colors in the crowd, I notice Brody doubled over, his hands on his upper legs. He looks ready to puke. We usually run close in our placement, though I didn't see him during the race.

Coach approaches Brody with a First Aid kit in hand. He sprays some disinfectant on Brody's leg above the front of his ankle. So Brody probably got spiked. *Too bad.*

I walk back to where our drivers' chairs are clustered and fish around in my gear bag for a water bottle. Others from the team drift over, looking spent, like there is nothing left in their leg muscles to keep them upright. I catch Ben's eye, and he gives a thumbs up. He must have done okay. Cole hangs with some girls just a little beyond the registration table. He travels with an entourage even at this hour of the day? If he's hit his average time or better, our team has a shot at the top spot.

Coach urges Brody to move. When he motions for help, Ben and I hurry over, put our shoulders under Brody's arms, and help him. If he can't walk it off, he'll stiffen up and feel even worse.

"What happened?" I ask, eyeing the four-inch square bandage just above his ankle.

"What does it look like?" Brody snarls, but I don't take the bait.

Ben and I haul him around until Coach waves us over to join the team.

"We did very, very well." Coach reads our unofficial times out loud from his clipboard. "Very nice numbers, gentlemen. Very nice! I'll have the postings when the finals are certified." Then he turns serious.

"On the down side, Brody got spiked on the last turn. I want everyone to stay here while I get the decision." He starts to leave, turns, and adds, "Start hydrating now, if you haven't already." With that, Coach hurries off to the officials' table.

Ben turns to me. "I heard what happened," he says in a low voice. "At the beginning of the fourth turn, Brody was making his move in a pack. He was behind someone from Lakewood and actually ran into the guy's spikes. I think if he gets disqualified, it'll be for what he said after he was nailed."

All runners are tired near the end of a race, so it would have been easy enough for Brody to bump into someone on a turn. Still, using foul language can be grounds for immediate disqualification. It depends on the circumstance, what was said, and who heard it.

Coach stands with the Lakewood coach and two officials who do all the talking. Then both coaches say something to each other and shake hands. Coach has a look on his face that my dad calls "inscrutable." This could go either way for Brody.

"I have good news, and I have bad news," Coach says, looking a lot less pleased than he was only minutes earlier. "The good news is that we won the meet." He grins as everyone roars and jumps up and down! A five-team invitational win is big for us.

Coach waits until we calm down. "The bad news is that Brody has been disqualified for language. A Lakewood runner was also disqualified for responding. Now listen to me: I don't want this to ever happen again. Not ever." He glares at Brody who slides a finger along his pressed lips and pretends to throw away a key. *Yeah, right. Like that will so happen.*

Then Coach's lopsided smile returns. "Most of you guys bettered your times today. I really like what I saw out there. You ran smart. Okay, let's move. I'm buying ice cream on the boat, so don't be late."

The storm has passed. But I wouldn't want to be in Brody's shoes at Monday's practice.

• • •

It's just after noon by the time we return to the island. Ben drives us to my house. My dad comes over to the car, still holding the shears he's been using to trim the front laurel. Ben turns the Honda off, and we give Dad the meet highlights. He smiles and claps his hands over his head when he hears our improved times.

Ben and I lean against the car as Dad asks Ben about the classes he plans to take at the U in January. My mind slides to Mackie and our previous evening. As Ben climbs back in the car to leave, I manage to get it together. "Hey, thanks for the ride. It was good today. Yeah?"

The corners of Ben's mouth turn up. Even his eyes crinkle upward. "Very good," he replies.

In the house, I head for the kitchen and open the refrigerator door. I am assessing the food on the shelves and trying to decide when I should call Mackie, when Justin walks in.

"You making lunch?" he asks, a hopeful note in his voice.

"Yeah, sure. Mom's gone until dinner, right?"

"That's what Dad said."

"How 'bout we grill hot dogs. This could be our last chance," I add, thinking about the months of impending winter rain. In October, a damp wetness usually begins that can last until the end of June.

"Did you run this morning?" Justin asks, eyeing my warmups.

"Yeah, we won."

"Cool."

Justin is the cool one. Nothing fazes him. He can laugh about almost anything. In that way, he is different than me.

I pull out a few slices of cheese to nibble on before lighting the grill on the outside porch. As we move outside, Justin swipes a slice and I pretend to chase him.

"Food Monster!" I yell at him. "Don't make me come after you, monkey boy."

I grab Justin by his shoulders and wrestle him to the ground, but my being forty-five pounds heavier calls for at least token handicapping. Justin laughs and tries to pin me. He's always pleased to prolong our roughhousing. We don't play for long though, as my thoughts return to Mackie. *What is she doing? What happened at the shelter today?* And there was that first kiss . . .

Dad approaches the grill, nodding his approval.

"Hey, add a couple of dogs for me," he says.

I slap two more hot dogs on the still-heating grill, return to the kitchen, and dump a can of baked beans in a pot. Justin takes out mustard, ketchup, relish, and plates, and sets them on the table. Dad pulls a large pitcher of lemonade from the fridge and pours three full glasses.

We demolish the food. When Justin emits a bullfrog-worthy belch, I laugh. Dad gets the hiccups. Justin begins belching in time to Dad's hiccups. That sends us over the edge. I laugh up tears.

Justin eyes my half glass of lemonade and makes a big 'Food Monster' face. He gives his best fake-evil laugh, "Heh, heh, heh." I drain the rest of my lemonade in three swallows.

After we clean up, I climb the stairs to take a shower.

"Justin," I hear Dad call. "I'd like some help putting those branches I cut in the truck."

I decide it might be a propitious (thank you, Mrs. Littlejohn, for that highly useful word) time to call Mackie. With Dad and Justin out of the house, my call will be private.

Lounging on my bed, I pick out her number on my phone.

"Hi, Jeremy," she answers in a melodic voice that makes me melt further into my mattress.

"Hey, Mackie. What's up?" It feels great just to hear her voice.

"How'd it go this morning?"

"We won. Ryan came in first, Cole was fourth, and I ran my best time," I almost add that Brody got spiked, but check myself.

"You do sound happy. Are you going to Jen's party tonight?"

"Yeah, sure."

"It's a sleepover for us girls, but you guys are invited for awhile."

"What time?"

"Around eight."

"Okay, see you there. And hey, it was nice last night. Good. On the porch," I say.

"Yes. It was."

After talking with Mackie, I shower and put on a pair of old warmups. Then I sneak in a nap on the canvas hammock on our back porch. While daydreaming about Mackie, I drift off to the fuel-deprived sputtering of our neighbor's lawn mower.

When I wake, it's to the touch of Mom's hand on my shoulder. The sunlight has grown dim.

"Jeremy, dinner's ready."

"Okay."

"I heard you had a big day."

"It was so fine," I mumble.

"Come in."

I walk into the kitchen. The table has been set and Mom and Dad are busy at the counter.

"Would you find Justin and tell him dinner's ready?" Dad asks when he sees me. I climb the stairs to the loft landing, legs feeling a bit stiff. Justin pops out of his room.

"Hey," I say.

"Are we having dinner now?" he asks, working on untangling his earbud wires.

"Yeah. Chicken."

Justin makes clucking sounds and then grabs his neck as if choking.

I trail him down the stairs. Once we're in the kitchen, the smell of baked chicken and garlic bread has us both focused completely on the food.

I pour glasses of milk for my brother and myself. Then, with very little conversation, we eat.

Mom is quiet, typical for her on a Saturday after she's taught most of the day. But midway through dinner, she asks, "Are you celebrating with the team?"

"No. Brody got spiked. Nobody wants to be around him tonight."

"Are you staying home?"

"No. Jen's asked everyone over."

"Who's going to be there?" Mom questions.

"The usual. Erica, Jon, Ty, Wes, Wendy, Mackie . . . maybe some others. I don't know. It's a sleepover for the girls."

"Who's driving?"

"Not sure. I'll probably catch a ride with Wes."

"Let me know who's driving before you leave, please."

I nod.

"Will Jennifer's parents be home?"

"Yeah. What's with all the questions?" I snap.

Dad answers. "After Spooner's last party, we want to know who's going to be at Jen's. You know some of the kids who were at Spooner's when the police showed up."

"So?" I ask, not following his point.

He looks at Mom then turns to me again. "Your mom and I don't want any surprise calls from the police. Not ever."

I shrug. They don't have to worry. I'm not going to end up like Spooner.

"It won't be that kind of party. The worst that might happen is that Jen and the girls will want us to dance." I grimace.

Mom raises her eyebrows.

"She has electronic games and we'll play cards. Don't worry, there won't be any drugs or vile alcoholic spirits," I add.

Dad sends me a look that says he'll hold me to every word. Can I ever reassure them enough?

"Do we have any dessert?" Justin asks, and the mood at the table shifts.

Mom nods. "Carmen gave me some peanut brittle today at school. She makes the best."

Justin seems interested but I shake my head, and pull out my phone to call Wes.

"Wes, can I catch a ride with you to Jen's tonight?"

"Hey, no problem, I'll see you around eight," he responds.

I tell Mom Wes will drive. *When will Mackie arrive at Jen's party?*

• • •

There's never any mistaking Wes' arrival. The low growl of downshifting as he approaches the house and slams to a fast stop on our gravel drive is a dead giveaway. I walk out to meet him, admiring his car, a hand-me-down, 5-speed, dark blue BMW from his mother.

"Hey."

Wes bobs to the music radiating from his speakers. He lives to listen to music. "*Hola!* Hey, you missed a great session last night. Fist was the best. They played about halfway through and everyone was up. Lots of girls, too. Yeah, it was good." Wes blisses on about a battle of the bands he went to hear in Seattle.

"Was anyone there from the island?" I ask.

"Couple of seniors with Spooner. They looked pretty messed up. Seemed like Beardsley's little brother was taking care of them."

"What do you think they were doing?"

"Who knows? Who cares?"

I shift in my seat. Wes has a point. Who cares? Drugs aren't our thing. They never have been.

After driving south for a few minutes, we turn at a numbered marker into Ty's driveway.

Ty has been Wes' and my good friend since grade school. He waits for us on the front porch of his parent's shrub-encircled home with Bouncer, a two-year-old bull terrier with an attitude. Ty and Bouncer run to Wes' car.

"Hey, Bounce, you can't come with us," Ty says as he opens the back door. Bouncer advances like he's going to jump into the car, but Ty heads him off and picks him up. Ty goes through the same routine whenever we pick him up. He explains that we're leaving and Bouncer is staying, as he gently carries his dog inside the house.

Ty jogs back to us and sits in the seat behind me. He's my height, so he has to fold his legs into his chest.

"Hi. Sorry. You know how much he likes to go for rides." Ty says in a rush.

"Yeah, we know," Wes says as he eases the car into second.

Ty nudges the back of my seat with his knee. "Jer, how'd it go today?"

"I got my best time," I reply, trying to keep the sound of boasting out of my voice.

"Yeah!" Wes says.

"What about the team?" Ty asks.

"We took the meet. Brody got disqualified for using foul language."

Both Wes and Ty hoot. Brody hasn't scored many 'friend' points with the underclassmen.

For the remaining eight minutes of our drive to Jen's house we mourn our school's dismal football prospects. Our team plays in a Seattle league that includes some big-name schools with lots of All State players. Soltrice High's football teams don't win very often.

Wes pulls off the road onto a dirt-packed drive marked by a red mailbox. Thick fir woods surround Jennifer's parents' home. It's lit up like a glowing ball in the cool evening. As we approach the porch, there's a shriek of laughter above the music, followed by Jen's voice encouraging everyone to dance. We head in anyway.

Inside we stand in a room that's about fifty by thirty feet. At one end is a kitchen, where soft drinks and snacks have been set out. But the main room is dedicated to old editions of Dance Station. Some of our friends gyrate, bounce, and laugh to the high-energy music. Girls and guys cluster near the music and screen, cheering the competing dancers.

Jen waves us over. "You gotta mooove," she sings, merging with the flow of the rhythm and choreography on the big screen at the end of the room. This is how Jen starts all of her parties: immediate dancing. Ugh. Wes, Ty, and I break into spastic moves, laughing at each other, like always.

Right away I spot Mackie at the far end in the kitchen, talking with Erica. I want to ask her about her day at the shelter. And I want to kiss her again just as much. Okay, more.

Mackie catches my eye and gives me a big smile. There's something about her smile that makes me feel like we're alone in that room of people. I wave to Wes and Ty and point to the kitchen. The guys continue crazy dancing as I cross the room, pulled to Mackie's side.

"Hi," I say to Mackie and Erica. "You're sitting this one out?"

"Oh, don't worry," Erica responds. "Jen has all kinds of kinky things planned tonight. I think she's counting on you guys to provide the entertainment."

I try to adjust my face into a horrified mask and ease into a zombie-like dance shuffle. Erica giggles. We both know it's a joke. Jen has never made any of us feel uncomfortable. She just likes to dance.

Mackie smiles faintly. "Hi. Yeah, we've been waiting for you guys," she says, playing along with Erica's teasing.

Mackie looks sleek tonight. To start with, her dark brown, red-flecked hair is long and loose. She wears a soft shirt that shows off all of her curves, which makes me crazy. How can I keep my eyes off of her or not want to fold her in my arms again, after last night?

My inner lust-boy thoughts are interrupted when Erica screams and runs to join the dancers. *Must be her song.* Mackie edges closer to me. We're alone.

"I have to do something tonight, and I need your help, okay?" she asks in a new, business-like tone.

"Uh, okay, what do you have in mind?" I reply.

"I need to go home."

"Why?"

"I'll explain, but first I'm going to tell Jen that we're going for a walk."

"Sure."

Mackie leaves me, plunging into the arm-flailing group of dancers. I am confused. She's gone from playful to serious in under thirty seconds. It will take us a half-hour to walk to her house. And a half-hour back. What's so important that she has to leave now?

In about a minute, Mackie returns. We exit through the front door as twenty-some pairs of eyes follow us. *Uh-oh.* Our early departure together isn't going unnoticed.

Outside, Mackie starts walking up the drive and I fall into step with her.

"We have to hurry."

"You mean like run?" I ask.

"No, maybe jog so I can keep up with you," she says, as if I would speed away.

"What's going on?" I ask as we break into an easy trot.

"I need to get to the water. Please, I don't know why. It's like something's pulling me there," she whispers, her words cutting off as her breath comes faster from our pace.

"What do you mean, *pulling?*"

She shakes her head, and we jog silently on the soft road shoulder. It's evening, close to nine o'clock, but a nearly full moon lights our way. Immediately upon arriving, we hurry down the first set of stone steps behind Mackie's house that lead to the seawall.

"Wait," she says, and we pause at a large storage box located at the stair's halfway turn.

Standing quietly, Mackie looks out at the water, searching to her left and right. I can't see anything in the waves.

"Do you see something?" I ask.

She doesn't answer for a moment then says, "We need the kayaks."

We remove life vests from the storage box and slip them on before continuing down the steps. From the racks built above the seawall, we lift out two sea kayaks and move to the shoreline.

"What's going on?" I ask.

She says nothing.

We place our kayaks at the shore edge and survey the water. The edgy stress radiating from Mackie earlier has evaporated. She's more focused.

She stands for a few minutes and then says, "I need to go out there. You don't have to. It'll be okay," she adds and then, without removing her sandals, steps in the water.

Fastening the clasps on my vest, I silently enter the cold water too, my wet jeans slowing me as I pull my kayak alongside hers. We walk, pushing our kayaks out far enough for them to float and then climb in. I've kayaked since I was five years old, so keeping my balance is easy, the way rolling out of bed and standing up in the morning feels instinctive.

We paddle side by side, without speaking until we're about two hundred feet from the shoreline. No one knows that we're out on the water. Mackie's parents are in Seattle, attending a symphony. Her sister, Noelle, has gone to a friend's house for the night. It could be kind of romantic to be out with her under the flooding moonlight. Except something else seems to be going on.

Suddenly Mackie stops, and motions for me to do the same. We float like two specks in the wrinkled nighttime waves.

Then, I see him! *Orcinus orca.* A black and white killer whale spy-hops about one hundred feet from us! He rises out of the water vertically, emits a low bellow, and then sinks slowly below the waves. My heart pounds. I tighten the grip on my paddle. He shouldn't be this close to shore. Or to us. This feels all wrong.

Mackie whispers, "Stay where you are." She guides her kayak so that she's about ten feet in front of me, facing into the Sound. Then she sets up, placing her paddle on the kayak's hull.

The whale surfaces again, using his tail to thrust himself up, this time clearly looking at us. Mackie remains perfectly quiet, focused on where the whale has shot up. Nothing on the water moves for maybe a minute.

Suddenly, standing high, he leaps out of the water almost on top of us. Only twenty feet away at the most! It's the spy move again. Holding his head above the waves, his eyes fix on Mackie as he groans! I can't breathe. We're sitting meat. He could kill us!

But Mackie doesn't move. The concentric waves from the orca's water displacement flow around her kayak. I'm set up the same way, and the waves ripple around me, too.

The whale bobs up and down five times, slowly, always concentrating on Mackie. Her head never turns away from him. Then he disappears under the surface. We wait. I'm going to break my paddle, I'm holding it so tight. *What if he's under us?* He emerges again several hundred feet away, and with a final slap of his flipper fins puts on a show of three diving leaps, and he's gone.

I watch in total wonder as he disappears.

"That was unreal," I call out. Then I notice she's slumped over the front of her boat. "Mackie!" I dip my paddle furiously and tear alongside her. She's too quiet: arms stretched out in front of her, hands resting loosely on her paddle. She's scaring the bejeezus out of me.

"Mackie?" I ask, my voice skating off the water. "Are you okay?"

She pushes up a little against the kayak's deck, only to slump down again.

"Shhh," she says in a shaky voice, "I need a minute."

So we sit under the loud moon glow. I turn my paddle over and over in my hands, worried. Mackie lies against her kayak's deck, really out of it. After what has to be at least ten minutes, she pushes herself up and, not looking at me, gingerly turns her boat around. Because the tide has been with us, we've floated close to shore. I paddle just behind her, keeping my eyes glued to her back, watching her progress.

Once near the shoreline, I ease in next to her. When she turns to look at me I see that her face is drawn and she's exhausted, like she's just finished running a hard race, flat out.

"Sorry. I guess I need some help," she says.

I slip out of my boat and pull it onto the beach. Then I return to Mackie, wading back in the calm shore water and bend down so she can leverage herself against me. It takes a while, but finally she's upright. I slip my left shoulder under her right arm and half drag her to the beach. She sits on the cold, wet sand and cobblestones with her head down in her hands.

Returning to the water once more, I haul her kayak out and place it on the rack.

I check in with her again. "Are you okay?" I ask, needing to have some idea whether she can walk.

"Yeah, thanks. I think it's going be a few minutes before I can get up the stairs." But, her eyes beg me for help.

I think about that as I put our paddles and vests back in storage. As I approach Mackie, I see her shaking even harder than when we climbed out of our boats. I don't have a jacket to give her so I sit on the ground, holding her against my chest, hoping my body will warm hers.

"Mackie, I've seen orcas hunting for food before, but this was the closest I've ever been to one. He was huge! I'm thinking thirty feet. We had six tons of whale next to us."

"Yeah, he was big. And really sick. I need to get some dry clothes on. So do you," she says.

I help her to stand. I want to ask her more about the whale. *Not now*, her eyes tell me.

Moving wouldn't be fast, I know that right off. I'm afraid to let go of her because her balance isn't good and she might fall over. So, I keep an arm around her. I feel Mackie's weight against my side.

We retrace our steps up the rough stone stairway and enter the Spence's house through their back door. Gus, the family's basset hound, greets us with nose bumps and follows us to the kitchen.

She looks at me and lets out a big sigh. "Will you call Jen?"

"Why?"

"Tell her that I'm not feeling well, that you walked me home, and you're going home, too."

I send a text to Jen:

mac not feeling 2 well I walked her home & am going home sorry 2 miss UR party

In a few seconds, I read Jen's reply:

2 bad. Miss U B good.

Mackie looks at the kitchen clock. It's close to ten. With one hand on the kitchen counter, she appears to have more strength, but occasionally shakes in an uneven shudder. "Sorry. I just don't want anyone to worry when we don't go back to the party," she says.

"Yeah, I can understand that."

"Jer, I have to take a shower or I won't warm up. If you want, you can too, in the guest room."

I know the house well. The guest bedroom and bath are just off the main room.

She calls after me. "Use the bathrobe on the shelf and meet me in the kitchen. I'll put your clothes in the dryer. Okay?"

"Okay," I say, still feeling like I'm in some play where I don't know my role. What is going on with Mackie tonight, and why am I part of it?

The spray of shower water registers hot against my chilled skin. My body soon is warm and relaxed, but my mind races. What if her parents come home early? How can we explain any of this? I quickly towel dry and put on a large, white bathrobe, wondering if Mackie has finished taking her shower.

Padding to the kitchen with my wet briefs, jeans, and shirt clutched in front of me like an offering to the dryer gods, I see Mackie standing next to two steaming cups.

I swallow hard. She looks so beautiful, her hair long, already dried and shiny, a light blue T-shirt bringing out color in her cheeks. She wears a pair of old, faded blue jeans that have patches on the back pockets.

"I didn't know if you wanted some, but I made us hot chocolate. I'll set the dryer on extract and speed dry," she says.

I hand her my soggy clothes. She turns the corner into a hallway, disappearing while I take my first sip of hot chocolate. It tastes so good I could gulp the scalding liquid and be finished before she's back.

She returns within seconds. I sit on a padded bar stool at the kitchen counter and turn to face her. Mackie walks right to me and I put my arms around her as she lays her head on my shoulder. She's still, not saying anything, just hugs me close.

After a while, she turns her head and kisses me on my neck near my ear. I tense at the feeling of her lips on my skin, and shift so I can kiss her. Time gets lost for both of us.

Then the dryer buzzer sounds and she backs away, leaving me somewhere between wanting more and amazed that anything has happened at all.

Before she leaves the room to respond to the dryer signal, she turns back to me.

"I have to thank you for what you did," she begins.

I wave my hand and shake my head.

Still looking at me, she continues. "I'm sure that the whale was what was pulling me to the shore. I didn't know that when we left Jen's, or what would happen. As soon as we were near the water, I knew something was coming to meet us. He was so sick." She waves her hand as if pushing away at cobwebs. "I'll get your clothes and we can talk."

As she left, I suck in a deep breath. *What a night!* And it's not over yet. Will Mackie tell me what all of this means?

She returns and hands me my warm clothes. My jeans feel a little stiff from saltwater, but dry.

I walk to the guestroom, dress, and head back to the kitchen. I find Mackie waiting in the great room, her hands clasped in front of her, eyes closed. When she opens them, she looks me over carefully like she's studying something about me.

"What?"

"Come on," she says, and leads me up the stairway to the second floor of the house.

She turns at her bedroom. I've been in her room many times over the years, but always with our friends. One time, when we were nine, everyone played on the floor with glass and agate marbles her father gave her. When the game was over, and as the others left to go home, she motioned for me to stay. She held out a milky-blue lutz marble with wavy gold ribbon edged in white. Mackie smiled at me, and time seemed to slow down; there was something close between us as she handed me the beautiful ball. It still makes me feel like we share something special.

Her room has been redecorated and looks quite different now, with dark green walls and long, brown and green velvet drapes covering the windows. A tall, ornately carved wood and glass cabinet has been positioned off to one side, with shelves that hold baseball-sized crystals. I recognize them as part of a rock and mineral collection that used to be in Nick Spence's home office. Mackie's room doesn't look at all girly anymore; it looks more like an enchanted forest.

"We can talk here," she says.

I stand mute, unsure of what to do.

Looking at the other side of the room, I notice her bed is still fitted with the fan like, seashell-shaped headboard she'd had as a girl. Her desk holds her notebook, school bag, some old books stacked in piles, and a red leather box, overflowing with bracelets. Above the desk are an antique oval mirror and a board with photos. I recognize some of the group prints from when we were kids.

Mackie takes my hand and tows me to the bed. "I want to tell you what I think happened tonight." She sits on the edge of the bed and then stretches out on her side taking up half of the space. "I'll share," she says, smiling, handing me a pillow. I flash back to childhood summer pillow fights with our friends. Then she scoots further across the bed, looks up at me, and says, "There's plenty of room."

Not knowing what she has in mind, I lie next to her and nod. At the same time, I try to contain my excitement. That doesn't work. Mackie raises her eyebrows and gives me a grin. I smile back, feeling embarrassed. She's seen all of us guys with woodies at some point over the years. This is different. This is just the two of us.

She puts her right hand on my arm. Surprisingly, her touch makes me relax.

"You heard the orca groaning, right? I think he was full of toxins."

I nod.

"I can tell you what it felt like to me, and what I think happened. But you have to promise that you won't talk about this with anyone. Okay? It will sound too crazy," she says, worry in her eyes.

"I promise."

"At Jen's, I was fine until just before you showed up. Then, I started to get this odd feeling like something was pulling at me. Kind of like when you hold the end of a vacuum cleaner hose close to your skin and the air sucks and pulls.

"I knew I had to leave, that I had to pay attention to that feeling. It seemed like it came from the direction of my house, so I decided to follow it. When we started walking, the vacuum pressure increased. That's why I asked if we could run. It was like I needed to get there, faster and faster.

"I could tell the pulling came from the water. But I didn't know how far out. The kayaks at least put us closer. When the orca surfaced, I knew. He was in trouble, and he was alone. He'd left his pod to find me. I needed to help him. So I waited until he could stay close to us."

I nod.

"He kept surfacing and looking at me. That started the connection between us. I couldn't have left, even if I wanted to. He felt stronger every time he looked at me."

I could feel my eyes opening wider, and my muscles tensing.

"Mackie, this is really ah . . . different," I say. "What did it feel like for you?"

She pauses and bites her lower lip.

"Once we made eye contact, I was locked in to him. Then, my energy moved to him. In the end, I couldn't move. Not even to paddle."

I'm fascinated. I've never heard anything before like what she's describing. And she can't be making it up. Everything fits with what took place around us. I saw most of it from behind her, in my kayak. She hadn't moved at all, until after he left.

"You remember that last series of dives? He was thanking me. It was so weird. I helped him, and he tried to give me something back. It sounds bizarre, I know." She shakes her head.

"So after he left, I lost it for a while. I'm really glad you went out with me." Her eyes stay on mine for my reaction. I feel overwhelmingly protective of her in this moment. I won't let anything bad happen to her.

Mackie cuddles into me, resting her head against my chest and putting her arm around my back. I hope I can stay cool, okay *respectful*, because she still seems kind of fragile from our time on the water. She resumes speaking, this time not looking at me.

"I had the same feeling when our boat capsized this summer. I was in the water getting really cold. Then, it felt like whatever happened, I would be okay. It was peaceful. And tonight, when the orca was with us, I felt the same way. Does this sound psycho to you? Who would think about jumping in the water with a whale?" She looks up at me.

I smooth her hair. "I don't think you're mental. I was there the whole time and you didn't do anything weird. The whale was awesome. So were you. How did you know what was wrong with him, that he was sick and needed you?"

"I'm not sure. I just knew. And I knew that all I had to do was keep my eyes on his. Then I felt drained, and when he left his energy was really big."

Now I can't help myself. I begin kissing her hair, and my lips stray down to hers. She breaks out of our kiss with a low sigh.

"Jer, the way the animals at the shelter have been and now this whale, I think that has to be related somehow. I've heard Doc talking with Gabe about how fast the animals have been healing. I feel funny, like I'm boasting. But you're the only person who's asked me about it."

"Right," I say. "The animals pay attention to you like they're waiting for something. They show you a lot of respect. It's like you're everyone's alpha. They don't do that with the rest of us. And Gabe's been the shelter's director for a long time, so he would see the accelerated healing. The animals do seem to recover faster after you've been with them. Do you have that same drained feeling when you leave the shelter?"

She thinks my question over. "Well, not nearly as much as I felt with the whale, but I've been pulled to animals and, after I've been with them, I feel kind of zapped."

We stay quiet for a minute or so, mulling over what she's said.

"I have another question," I say.

"No, not another," she teases.

"Uh, why is this happening, now? Or, has it been happening but you haven't noticed it before?"

"That's two questions. Two good questions. I don't know. And I've thought about it a lot. Why me? It's not like I asked for this."

So she's been trying to figure things out all along. I want to stay and talk with her all night. I check my watch. It's just eleven.

Mackie's eyes have closed. *Has she fallen asleep?* I run my fingers through the ends of her hair. Her eyes open. She's wide-awake now.

"I'm sorry."

"It's fine," she says.

I pull her in closer, eliminating any space between us as a shiver runs up and down my body.

"You too?" she asks.

Yeah, me too. I smile, knowing what she means.

We hold each other, and this time I don't feel like I have to be embarrassed about my totally turned on reaction to her. There's no question about her knowing I think she's hot.

Finally, I say, "Hey, I need to be home by eleven thirty."

"Okay," she says, sleep rolling through her voice.

I swing my legs off the bed and sit up. If I'm too late, Jen's parents will get a worried call from my mom. I need to run to be home near curfew, but I can cruise for hours just off the excitement of the evening, especially the way I felt holding her.

Mackie walks me downstairs and watches as I torture my feet into my wet shoes.

Before I leave, she hugs me and says, with a mysterious smile, "I'll call you tomorrow. This time, I have a question for you."

CHAPTER 4

Sunday mornings have always been prime sleep time. On this Sunday, though, I wake at six thirty, my brain in overdrive.

Lying in bed, propped up on pillows with my notebook open, I list what I know to be true:

1. Animals respond to Mackie's presence by showing her respect and submission.
2. Mackie is pulled to sick and wounded animals through some kind of air vacuum.
3. Mackie either generates or accelerates animals' recoveries through an energy transfer.
4. Mackie feels tired or, in the case of the orca, drained, after being with a sick animal.
5. Mackie isn't frightened by what has been happening.

The orca and Mackie had a connection that I can't fully understand, but I recognized something when he surfaced to look at her. He wasn't a predator sizing us up for dinner. He'd seemed more like a whale who'd swum in to be with his best bud. How can the orca know Mackie? Is Mackie telling me everything she knows? And how can I see and verify all of it?

But Mackie trusts me. I know that because of the scar she has on her leg. Just two years ago, the summer of our freshman year, a group of us had decided to swim after hours in the East Point Country Club pool. It was mid-July and we'd been at the town square to hear a band playing. The country club was within a mile of the sound stage.

Six of us, Mackie, Jon, Wendy, Jennifer, Wes, and I, decided it would be cool to climb the club's wire security fence and take a moonlight dip in the outdoor pool. Starlight filtered through tree boughs as we stripped down to our underwear in the dim shadows. The girls giggled. We eased quietly into the pool water, enjoying relief from the summer heat. Suddenly, the overhead security lights blazed.

A voice boomed at us from the clubhouse porch. "I want everyone out of the pool. *Now!*"

We were busted! Hauling ass out of the water in high warble, we grabbed for our clothes, and hit the fence in wet underwear, scrambling to get over the enclosure. We got away before the police showed up, but the fence top was capped with twisted edges of metal. Mackie was cut just below her left knee. Blood streamed down her leg as we arrived at Jon's house. His parents were next door, visiting with their neighbors. We huddled like fugitives in the kitchen.

"Jon, could I have some paper towels and a piece of tape?" Mackie asked, holding a wad of tissues against the gash on her leg. Wendy and Jennifer looked at her like she was crazy.

"Mackie, that looks bad. We should go to the hospital," Wendy suggested.

"I'm not going anywhere," Mackie said.

Jon left the room and returned with a roll of paper towels and a First Aid kit.

When Mackie lifted the tissues, I saw that her wound was deep. Like needing-stitches-deep.

"Mackie, I think you should see someone for that," I said.

She looked up at me. "No. Then I'd have to tell Mom and Dad. How would I explain any of this? They'd ground me for the rest of the summer. And you guys might get in trouble, too."

"I don't think the bleeding's going to stop," Jon said, frowning. Jennifer, Wendy, and I nodded. Mackie shot us a defiant look.

"Okay, Jeremy," she said. "You sew it up."

At first I thought she was messing with me, but she didn't smile, just held my eyes in hers. Jon left to get his mother's sewing box.

Trying to recall how sutures were stitched at the animal shelter, I splashed isopropyl alcohol on a small needle and threaded it with white thread. Then, as Mackie watched me in silence, I washed the wound with the alcohol, sewed the split skin with seven small stitches, added antibacterial spray on top, and finally applied a layer of gauze bandages.

Mackie had tears in her eyes as I finished. I couldn't tell if they were from pain or relief. Before everyone left to go home, she pressed her hand in mine and said, "I owe you."

After last night, I now feel like I owe Mackie something. She paddled out to meet an orca whale that could have killed us with a flip of a fin. She isn't spooked by the idea of animals that somehow heal in her presence, even if she's not sure how the energy exchange thing works. And she trusts me with knowing all of it, trusts that I won't out her as some kind of freak show.

My skin tingles from the morning cold, and I tentatively set my feet on the braided rug next to my bed. It's early, but I need to move. My body is tightening down from the race yesterday and walking will help. Padding quietly in my sleep shorts, T-shirt, and bare feet down our wooden stairs, I hear Justin and Mom.

As I step into the kitchen, Mom looks up from the cantaloupe and honeydew melons she's chopping at the island counter. "Oh, I didn't expect to see you up this early. Are you okay?" she asks.

Mom, a morning person, is both alert and waiting for my answer.

"Yeah. Well, my legs feel kind of stiff. I need a banana."

Justin's eyes narrow as he watches me peel a banana before our customary late-morning, Sunday brunch.

I smile. Competition for food is basic to every animal household.

"Justin. You can have a banana, too," Mom says. She's a good primate mother who knows it's wise to diffuse signals of sibling jealousy.

He raises his eyebrows and wriggles them at me. I grimace back at him.

"Dad and I fell asleep reading before you came in last night. Did you have a good time at Jennifer's party?" Mom asks, as she returns to dicing the fruit.

Setting my hands on the counter and leaning forward, I stretch my leg muscles. Lots of runners' calf muscles cramp the day after racing and mine are getting there. Usually, eating something high in potassium, like a banana, helps.

"Oh, yeah, it was okay. Jen put on some old Dance Station." Luckily, Mom has heard abbreviated answers for years about what I do on the weekends.

"Hmmm. Well, what's going on with everyone? Is anyone dating?"

"Mom, people don't date anymore." I pause to reconsider. "Well, Jon and Erica are sort of seeing each other, but you know, that's different."

"Different? How?" she quizzes, looking up from chopping the fruit.

"They've liked each other since grade school. Everyone figures they'll end up an old married couple."

"An old married couple," Mom repeats with a chuckle. "Right." She turns to push melon rinds into our composting pail.

Moving out of my stretch, I slide into a pair of worn flip-flops by the kitchen door before turning to the oversized calendar on the bulletin board. The kitchen calendar shows all of our daily schedules.

"Are we marking up October today?" I ask, hoping to change the subject.

"Yes. You finish with cross-country soon, right?"

"Yeah. And I don't think Olivia will change my hours."

"Fine. Are you doing homework, or do you want to help with breakfast?"

"Homework, I guess," I respond. There isn't much choice. I have lots to read.

"Okay. I'll let you know when we're ready to eat." Mom waves me off.

"You know I'm going to the shelter around two o'clock, right?"

She nods and hands Justin a piece of cantaloupe to eat. He sends me a big grin, like he's just been awarded top prize.

Moving gingerly up the stairs, I try to get myself in study mode. My French, English, and history classes require extra time because I read slowly. I never have to spend nearly as much time on my chemistry or algebra homework. But my incentive to study that morning isn't nearly as strong as my desire to review what happened with Mackie. And I'm beyond curious for another reason. What question does she want to ask me? I space out and nap.

I jerk awake. With some relief, I hear Mom calling my name. It's around noon. She's made my favorites: pancakes, eggs, and fruit. After the meal I try to read more. Finally, at one forty-five I stroll to the wildlife shelter. I've packed in a lot of food and do not feel like running. It's enough to enjoy the light-blue sky and crisp, fall breeze.

Entering through the shelter's front door, I enjoy the memory of lying next to Mackie on her bed. My daydream is cut off when the door opens again. Mrs. Vartan and Dru McKibbon have arrived. We've been the Sunday afternoon team for the last eight months.

Like many of our shelter's volunteers, Mrs. Vartan is old, maybe over sixty. After her first husband died, she used to sail in all kinds of weather to her son's home on the north end. In the summer, they played croquet on the lawn and she'd take her grandson to the beach to skip stones.

Both of my grandmothers died when I was still a baby, so I enjoyed listening when she recounted taking young Hughie aboard her 24-foot sailboat, the two of them playing pirate as they sailed up and down Locke's Pass, raising their Jolly Roger flag, and waving to people on the shoreline. That would have been outstanding.

Dru is my age, but homeschooled, so I don't know her well. She started volunteering at the shelter a year ago. Occasionally the distress of the animals gets to her, but animals in pain get to all of us.

We review the day's workload. It's pretty light. No new injury admissions except for a peahen that someone shot and a young male coyote that was brought in the day before. Later, I'll ask Mackie if she already saw him when she worked yesterday afternoon.

I finish suiting up and wait for Dru to join me for our check-in. Afternoons are prime sleep time for animals because many are nocturnal. But when you factor in injuries, any bird, mammal, or reptile that's hurt requires sleep off and on, around the clock.

First, we look in on the peahen, *Pavo cristatus,* a domestic bird. That's a genus and species name that I don't get to see, or practice saying, often. She's been placed in a medium-sized cage in one of the rooms with some smaller birds. The feathers on the tip of her right wing have been damaged. A surgical envelope, shaped like a rectangular sleeve, has been slipped over the last five inches of her wing. She's been given a light sedative to quiet her. Her food and water bowls are still full. Soundlessly, we leave the room and close the door.

"Why would anybody shoot a peahen?" Dru asks in a whisper.

"Who knows? It's stupid. Her mate wouldn't have been too far away. If she came from near Hawke Harbor, I know the people that raise them. Have you ever seen the Henrys' peacocks?"

"No, but the males' feathers are gorgeous. I couldn't see the hen well. Do the females have any bright colors?"

"Not really. Mainly they're sort of brown and gray."

"Hmmm," Dru looks up at me with a giggle. "So the pea men are styling. Seems like the males are big show offs."

I grin at her. Male peacocks, with their deep-blue, iridescent green, and rust-colored feathers, compete to attract mates. When a peacock fans his tail he can make the males of any other species look downright dowdy.

We continue down the hall, looking in on sleeping animals through door windows. All is quiet. I try to concentrate on what's in front of me, but images of Mackie and the whale keep surfacing, like hallucinations.

Moving back to the main room, we rejoin Mrs. Vartan.

"That new coyote pup made a mess in Cage D this morning," she says, wrinkling her nose. "I heard Doc had to reset his back leg and the pup went bonkers when the team walked in. Probably the tranquilizer wasn't strong enough. He's in isolation right now, so would the two of you do the cleanup, please? I'll keep an ear open for the phone and clean out the small birdcage."

Dru and I nod and turn to the cleaning closet. We need buckets, disinfectant soap, and scrubbers. I also remove two respirator masks from the upper shelf.

"How stinky is this going to be?" Dru asks, eyeing the masks as we exit to the outside.

I hand her one. "You've never smelled coyote urine before?"

"No. It's bad, right?"

"Oh yeah," I reply as we round the bend to the fourth of ten outdoor cages.

Even with the advantage of fresh air and a breeze, the foul odor hits us like a wall. We set our cleaning materials down and quickly put on our masks. The base of the cage is splattered with feces. Other fluids have splashed on the open metal links and dried. Seeing how bad things look, I turn back to the main building. Before I put too much distance between myself and the cage, I lift my mask and motion for Dru to join me. She runs to my side.

"I need to get the pressure washer," I tell her quietly. "Don't do anything until I'm back."

It will be best to first power-spray everything from a distance, and cleaning will be a real challenge. Using their urine, coyotes mark territory to let each other, and other animals, know they're around. Farmers and gardeners sometimes buy and apply the urine concentrate to keep deer away. I can understand why it works. Stinkeroo! And we humans don't have nearly the acute sense of smell that wild animals have.

After the pressure wash we scrub, and in about ten minutes we take off our masks. The smell isn't as strong, but still foul. Dru pulls a face like she's about to gag, but handles it all pretty well. At least, she doesn't say anything. In twenty minutes the cage is clean, with Dru doing the final pressure-spraying to rinse everything off.

We've just returned the disinfectant and scrubbers to main storage in the shelter when I feel my phone buzz. It's a message from Mackie!

R U off at 6?

yes Y

Call me then, PLZ.

It's four o'clock and we still have more cleanup. Mrs. Vartan motions us over to the front desk.

"The Large Flight Cage didn't get cleaned this morning. They were short a volunteer and just ran out of time. Jeremy, would you handle that?" she asks.

I nod because I like being in the big cage with Number 26. Cleanup includes removing bird droppings and food scraps that haven't been eaten. Those can be almost anything. Like the hair or bones of dead, thawed chicks, rats, mice—whatever has been sent to the wildlife shelter. Though we breed mice for food, sometimes there isn't enough, and our director, Gabe Hawes, purchases "frozen dinners." We have an old microwave for defrosting the "dinners" before they are placed in cages for the birds to find. I remember watching in horror when a new volunteer took her warmed sandwich from the animal warming microwave to eat. Whoa! We have another microwave for our own food!

Mrs. Vartan continues. "Dru, let's transfer the new dry feed from the bags into the bins. Then we'll check the boxed donations that came in yesterday." The gifts will include old towels, linens, and bandaging items that people have dropped off.

With my hood and goggles in place, I approach the Large Flight Cage quietly. Afternoon is down time for Number 26. Eagles sleep at night, but are most active in the morning, when they usually hunt. Since Number 26 has been with us for about six months, she knows our schedule for cleaning this cage. If she wanted to, she could get territorial and come after me, but she never has before. A part of me wants to believe that she understands how much we've been trying to help her. Or maybe she doesn't and only tolerates us because of her weakened state.

Brody was lucky when Mackie moved into the cage to defend him. Yeah, Number 26 absolutely would have noticed Brody. With two centers of focus, eagles can see both forward and out to the sides of their eyes at the same time. When an eagle hunts, it spots small animals on the ground up to one and a half miles away. There is no way that anyone could sneak in and surprise Number 26.

My thoughts return to Mackie as I clean the cage. Mackie and Number 26. What has Mackie done that makes Number 26 show her respect? What is it about Mackie and wounded animals? How does the energy exchange work? What, exactly, does she do for them?

Exiting, and after locking the cage door, I pull off my hood and dump the eagle's refuse in a waste compost bin before heading back inside the shelter building. Re-entering the main room, I sit with Mrs. Vartan and Dru in a loose circle around the front desk.

We review new informational handouts that Gabe and Olivia have prepared about ospreys.

Finally, Mr. and Mrs. Keith, two volunteers who have worked third shift for a long time, push through the front door, laughing about something. I jump to my feet, ready to end the day. Mrs. Vartan nods. "You and Dru go ahead. I'll wait for Seth," she says smiling at us.

"Thanks," I return and then, "See you," to Dru. Passing the Keiths, I give them a big smile. It feels good to know that Mackie wants to talk with me.

Walking up the shelter entrance drive, I pull my phone out and call her.

"Hey, what's up?"

"Hi, where are you?" she asks, in a soft voice that gives me goose bumps.

"Heading home."

"Were there any emergencies?"

"None. It was really quiet."

We paused. Had I lost her?

"Jeremy, I should have asked you this a long time ago, but if you aren't already going to Sadie One, would you go with me?"

Somehow, I manage to hold onto my cell phone as I leap high in the air, pumping my fist. She has just asked me to the first of two Sadie Hawkins dances that our school holds every year. This is way better than I could have guessed.

"Yeah, sure, that would be great," I say, excitedly. Holding my cell phone an arm length away from my mouth, I make a disgusted face. That didn't sound very cool. Bringing the phone back, I try to sound more sophisticated by speaking in a lower octave, "I mean, yes, I'd like to go with you."

"Oh, good." She seems relieved. "It starts at seven thirty on Friday. That's when the Dance Club begins their clinic. They show everyone dance steps. It'll be like last year's Sadie One. Do you know how to dance to fifties music?"

"Not really. Will that make a difference?"

"No. It won't be as wild as dancing at Jen's, but it'll be fun. And guess what?" Her voice hits a conspiratorial tone. "I heard Angela Bruner asked Wes."

"Oh," I say, surprised. "Wes hasn't said anything."

"She asked him last night at the party. At least that's what Jen told me this morning."

"Okay. I didn't know Angela had a thing for Wes," I comment, perplexed as usual by the ins and outs of high school romance.

"Yeah. It's cool. Angela's pretty sweet and, well, you know Wes. He's fun. I think they could be good together."

I raise my eyebrows at her last statement. Wes has never seemed remotely interested in Angela. But I never thought I'd have a chance with Mackie, so hey, maybe Wes and Angela?

"Jeremy are you there?"

"Uh, yeah. Have you finished the French translation?" I ask, searching for a subject that will put me back on solid ground.

"No. Do you want to work on it together tonight, after dinner at my house?"

"That sounds good."

I stop at the top of our driveway. After saying goodbye to Mackie, I run full speed down the slope, bank the curve, and land on our porch in one leap. Opening the door, I body slam into Dad as he leaves the vestibule.

"Jeremy," he says, steadying himself against the doorframe. "What's the big hurry?"

"Sorry. Didn't see you coming out. When's dinner?" I ask, regaining my balance by grabbing the other side of the doorframe.

"I'm just about to take the corn off the grill and put hamburgers on. You hungry?"

"Of course," I grin. I'd better calm down. If my parents find out how happy I am about seeing Mackie, there could be all sorts of questions to answer. Questions that I want to avoid for all sorts of reasons.

Continuing into the kitchen, I find Justin holding our plastic ketchup and mustard bottles in front of him on the table, like pistols. He has set them up so I'm in their aim-line as I walk in.

"Don't even think about it, young man!" Mom advises.

Justin hee-hees and grins like an evil elf.

"Hey," I say to him. "What's shaking?"

He shrugs and sets the ketchup and mustard bottles upright on the table.

"Mom, how soon before we eat?" I call out.

"If I can get some help cutting these tomatoes and apples, about five minutes. Is that soon enough?" she responds, looking a bit stressed.

"Yeah, I can do that."

"Anything new today?"

"Someone brought in a peahen that was shot, and we have a coyote pup with a dislocated leg joint. They'll be okay. Otherwise, it was the usual," I say, moving past her to pick out several tomatoes lined up on a nearby windowsill.

I stand at the counter and cut two large, ripe tomatoes in thick slices for burgers. Then I quarter four apples, sneaking a pre-dinner snack.

"Justin," Mom says. "Dad forgot the cheese. Would you please take this out? Thank you," she finishes, as she transfers a small plate to his hands.

Looking like he carries the crown jewels of the kingdom, Justin bows his way out of the kitchen. Justin the Court Jester. I have to laugh.

Within a few minutes, Dad and Justin return with a platter of grilled corn, cheeseburgers, and toasted buns. As usual, once our food hits the kitchen, all activity becomes focused. Meaning we eat without saying much. We really aren't so different than the rest of the animal kingdom.

"Jeremy. Jeremy? Do you have homework to finish?" Mom asks.

"Oh, yeah." I respond in a deliberately casual manner. "Mackie and I are getting together tonight to translate a story for French."

Mom sends me a questioning look. "I didn't know Mackie and you had French class together."

"Yeah. I'll be home by ten."

Mom and Dad look at me like they have questions stuck on their lips. Dad clears his throat. He gets a faint smile on his face. I've seen this look before, but haven't quite figured it out.

"Just don't be too late," he says.

Justin reaches for an apple wedge and spills his milk. I could hug the little guy for his timely diversion.

After we finish, I take the stairs two at a time to my bedroom and pack my notebook. Then I race through a five-minute shower, put on a clean, dark blue T-shirt, and grab my fleece jacket. Moving at a fast jog, I arrive at Mackie's house at 7:22 P.M.

Mackie's fourteen-year-old sister, Noelle, answers my knock at the front door. She looks me up and down as if seeing me at her house is a special event.

"Hellooo, Jeremy, dear Jeremy" she trills like an opera singer. "I'll get Mackie."

Noelle slips up the stairs, long blonde hair swinging, as I remain just inside the Spences' front door.

From where I stand, I look east to a bank of windows facing the Sound. It's a panoramic view of water and the Cascade Mountains. The Seattle skyline will become visible once I move further into the room. Inside, the house holds a lot of old furniture, antiques from Mrs. Spence's family.

The Spences' house has been like a headquarters for my friends since we were kids, and our families met there after the sailing accident. Until Mackie returned home from the hospital, there was a steady stream of homemade dinners delivered to their door.

I know Mackie's father, mother, and sister almost like extended family. Nick Spence likes to have big barbecue parties with lots of friends. Originally from Georgia, he uses words that I can't always follow. He calls everyone Bud or Bub. I've always liked him.

Mackie's mother, Caitlin, is from Seattle. My mom said Caitlin comes from a wealthy family and Nick wouldn't have to work if he didn't want to, though he still does, as a salesman for an organic coffee company.

Before Mackie arrives, Mr. Spence walks out of the kitchen with Gus, at his heels.

"Hey, Bud, how're you doing?" Nick Spence asks in his thick southern drawl. He is a big man, standing about half a foot taller than me, and built like a pro linebacker.

"Fine, thank you," I reply. Has Mackie told her parents that we're studying together? Meanwhile, Gus noses forward for pats. I stroke his smooth coat and tickle his long jowls. He rewards me with grateful doggy slobber. Nick digs in his jacket pocket and hands me a paper towel for my hands.

"So you and Mackie are going to study tonight. I'm taking Gus here out for a little walk, but you make yourself at home now. Mackie will be right along. Gus, bud, come on! We got to get going."

With that, I am alone.

I walk into the great room to the wall of windows, looking at the Cascades. Most of the snow melted during the summer, and the range looks dark and forbidding. That will change in a month or two when the temperatures drop, and heavy, moist air plants snow on the peaks.

I have turned away from the windows to look back into the room when I hear Mackie say, "Hi. We can sit in here. Do you want a glass of water or something to drink?"

My heart thuds as I take her in. She wears jean shorts with light-colored suede ankle boots that show off her legs. A white shirt hangs down to cover most of her shorts. Brown and turquoise colored beads are on her wrist. Her dark, shiny hair flows straight down past her shoulders and swings as she moves toward me. She motions to a grouping of couches and armchairs clustered near the windows. I've sat there many times before with our friends, relaxed and comfortable. Now, I feel a little strange.

"Jeremy? Do you want some water?" she repeats.

"Hi, yeah, water is fine. Thanks," I manage to choke out.

Mackie moves into the kitchen and returns with two tall glasses of water and a plate of cookies.

"I like how you study," I note, looking at the cookies.

"You can thank Noelle. We don't always have homemade peanut butter cookies. She surprised everyone today. It's our Grandma Unis' recipe."

I nod, impressed.

We open our notebooks to a three-page story section for translation.

"We could write translations and then check each other's work," Mackie suggests.

"Sounds good." Great. It's already hard to stay focused. Sitting next to Mackie on the sofa reminds me of how it felt to hold her the night before. Bowing my head, I try to only think of what is in front of me on my notebook screen.

Mackie finishes the translation first and reaches for a cookie. I'm slower, but within a few minutes I do the same.

"Let's trade and use editing marks," she says.

Stuffing the rest of a cookie in my mouth, I set my notebook on the coffee table in front of us and take hers. Then she picks up my notebook. For the next ten minutes we review each other's assignment. I only have one comment about her work. Mackie always scores near the top in our class, and I can't find anything wrong in her translation.

We exchange notebooks again. I see she's questioned my use of a few articles. In French, all nouns are masculine or feminine. Words, like "a, an, the, this" have to agree with the gender of the noun they modify. Six of mine are wrong.

Mackie giggles when she reads what I wrote on her page.

We'd translated a story about a boy and girl visiting a French art museum, making comments about historical paintings. I asked if they really knew what they were talking about.

She deletes what I wrote, but I'm happy. I've made her laugh, and Mackie's laughter makes everything right. Her even, white teeth flash, and dimples appear in the sides of her cheeks. Best of all, her dark eyes lock onto mine. They're full of mischief.

Next, we take turns reciting the story. My pronunciation starts out clumsy, but in the end, we both do pretty well. Within an hour, we're finished. Mackie's father returns with Gus during our recitation, and they move to another part of the house.

"Let's go outside, on the deck," she suggests, picking up the cookie plate to take with us.

I slide the nearest set of heavy glass doors open and follow her out.

Dusk has settled. The sky has cleared, so the air feels a little chilly. Mackie sits near me on the outdoor sofa. I rest my arm along the top of the back cushion so she can snuggle in closer. She props her feet on the low table in front of us and I do the same. The contrast of cooled air to the warmth where we touch triggers an inner smile. Puget Sound water shimmers in front of us.

"Have you thought more about what happened last night?" I ask.

"What part of last night?"

"Yeah, well, it was all worth reviewing." I grin a little, not wanting to say how very, very much I've been thinking about our time together when we returned to her house. "I was thinking of the orca."

Her eyes blink like she's deciding how to answer.

"I still don't know why," she says. "I wish I did, but I don't. Today it all seems unreal. The whale being so close to us and feeling energy moving from me to him. It was like watching him recharge his batteries. Have you heard of anything like that?"

"No. Nothing even close."

"I went online and tried to find other people who have had this happen to them. I didn't find anything. Maybe people just don't talk about it. I mean, who would believe me if I told them what happened last night?"

"We don't have scientific corroboration for everything that happened, but I believe you accurately described what you experienced," I reply carefully.

"Yes, but you were there. And you understand," she says, sliding her left hand into my right so that our fingers entwine.

"Well, sooner or later, you'll know more. I think it's pretty big, whatever is going on." I want to stay here all night with her under the quiet sky. Drifting breezes off the saltwater mingle with the fragrance of Mackie's hair, floating two of my now-favorite scents. We sit quietly for a few minutes, drinking it all in.

She turns to face me. "Jeremy, you're good about going to the dance with me. Right?"

"Yeah, sure, better than good. But I have to ask you something. Will Brody have a meltdown?"

"He shouldn't. We haven't gone out since my accident in June. I told him I needed space and he shouldn't wait."

"It's not that I'm worried, but I'd like to know if he still thinks you have something going on," I say.

"There never was an 'us' really. Besides, he's seeing Jilly Parker now," she replies.

"Okay, just checking. I don't want to get into a turf thing with him."

"Has he said something to you? Because we're definitely over. I'm the one who ended it. If he has a problem, it's with me," she says and lifts her chin.

"Uh-huh, I'm not sure he'd see it that way," I mutter. "So do we have to get dressed up for the dance? I mean like fifties retro?"

"If we want to, but it doesn't matter. The Dance Club dresses up. You'll see some girls in wide skirts and some guys in skinny ties. I might put my hair in a ponytail. We'll have fun however we look."

With that, she leans over, picks up the cookie plate, and holds it out to me.

"Well, if I must," I say, and we both laugh. "These are really good. Noelle should bake more often."

As if on cue, Noelle emerges from the closest slider door and struts out to stand in front of us.

"What's going on out here?" she asks in a no-nonsense voice, then breaks down in giggles as she reaches for a cookie.

"Hey, lamb chop," Mackie replies in a teasing voice. "We just finished our homework, *ma petite*. What's up?"

"Nothing. What're you doing?" Noelle is full of phony innocence. I hope she doesn't plan on staying.

"We were having a little conversation about what a dear sister you are. How you have the best manners, and would never barge in on your sister when she's entertaining a young gentleman. La-dee-dah, you can't find sisters like you any more," Mackie carries on in a hokey, Southern accent.

I recognize this as a kind of game they have played for years. "Suffering Southern Belle Theater" their mother calls it. Nick will occasionally correct their 'Southern' dialect. The girls were born and raised in the Pacific Northwest and their father is the only true Southerner among them.

"Okay," Noelle looks at me under her lashes as she switches back to her normal voice. "Jeremy you do know that I made these cookies?"

"Yes," I answer in my best guy-gets-right-to-the-point voice. "Mackie told me."

"Oh. Well, do you like them?" Noelle seems determined to stay with us.

"They are so good that we may have to take you down to the beach for a 'thank-you' dunk," I reply, keeping a straight face.

Noelle clutches her hands to her chest and pretends to be frightened. The girl loves drama.

"That's a good idea," Mackie says, standing up.

Noelle runs, shrieking, into the house.

"Actually, going down to the beach is a very good idea," Mackie repeats, looking at the door where Noelle has disappeared. "I'll be back in a minute."

When she returns, she has a sweater on and holds my jacket out to me.

Much like the previous night, the moon lights the sky. It's nearing the end of September and our warm Indian summer days will soon be overtaken by chilly rain. Clear evenings like this are special. On nights like this, for the last three years, Mackie has asked our friends to her house for a moonlight paddle. I usually stay next to her on the water.

Mackie precedes me down the cement block steps to the beach, and I can't help but compare this night with the evening before. What if another whale needs her to go out in the water? How long can she keep this from her parents, or anyone else?

I don't have time to worry. When we move off the last step, Mackie puts her arm around my waist. I do the same with her. We meander through a course of dark, rounded rocks and smooth stones pushed in by the tide. She seems more relaxed the further we get from the house. We joke about Noelle's dramatic timing.

"Mackie," I say, changing the subject, "you do know that everyone saw us leave Jen's together last night?"

"Yeah. When Jen called today she asked about it. I told her that I wasn't feeling well and you walked me home."

"Okay, but what about the dance? Did you tell Jen we're going together?"

She frowns. "Not yet. Let's tell everyone at lunch tomorrow. I'll do it. Are you okay with that?"

"Sure. What about your mom and dad? Will they think it's weird that you invited me? I mean we haven't done anything like this before. You know, together."

"They've always liked you. I know they'll be happy that we're going to the dance." She pauses. "Are you worried about your parents? What they'll say about me asking you?"

"No. Well, my mom may get kind of excited. I think she might have been into dances when she was growing up."

We're quiet for a few minutes and move past the Spence's property line. The tide is still way out so we continue. Sound tidelands aren't easy to walk, with wet, coarse-grained, spongy sand littered with small rocks and stones. Our progress is slow, in time with the distant lapping sound of the water.

"Have you ever felt like you had to go to an animal when we've been in school, or maybe during dinner with your family or something?" I ask.

"That hasn't happened. I guess it could, though. Last night it didn't feel like I had a choice."

"Maybe it won't be a problem." I notice the smile has left her face.

"You know, I'm not going to stop living my life because of this. If it doesn't go away, it will just have to be part of who I am. Are you okay with that?" she asks, stopping our walk.

"Mackie, I'm very good with who you are," I say, searching for her eyes in the dim light. "I'll help whenever you need me to."

Then she hugs me, and we kiss in the moonlight, and it all seems too good to be true.

Chapter 5

At school Monday morning, as I stow clean running gear in my locker, someone moves in next to me. Wes.

"Hey," I say, not looking at him.

"Hey," he echoes in an excited voice. "So what happened with you and Mackie after you left Jen's house?"

I have a feeling this is just the beginning of lots of questions about Mackie and me.

"She didn't feel well so I walked her home," I say, sticking to Mackie's script.

"Yeah, it looked like something else."

"What did it look like?'

"Like maybe you and Mackie have a little something going on. You two ditched pretty early."

"Who's saying that?" I demand, hoping he hasn't been spreading some kind of story around. I don't want to be the center of gossip.

"Everyone saw you leave together. Like right after we got there. And you never came back. Hey, Mac's into you, man."

"What makes you think she's into me?"

"She laughs at your lame jokes."

I sock his arm, but not very hard.

"She did have a question for me," I say.

"Yeah, what was that?"

Oops. Wes is way too interested, and I don't want to explain that Mackie and I are going to Sadie One together. I promised her she could tell everyone.

"Gotta go," I say looking at the hall clock. "See you at lunch." I feel Wes' puzzled eyes on my back as I walk away.

It's a struggle to stay focused in class, even though I'm aware that Mr. Wakely likes to prowl around the room as he speaks, looking for students who aren't paying attention.

"Okay, let's see what you learned from today's assignment . . . Who can tell me the name of the Confederate commander at Fort Sumter?" Mr. Wakely pauses, his eyes searching for a victim. "Mr. Tarleton?"

Hearing my name, I have a moment of panic. Did I hear the full question? I suck in a deep breath and take a chance, "General Beauregard."

"Correct. Now, someone tell me the name of the Union commander," he demands moving on to another victim. "Mr. Hirshfeld, who was the Union's commander?"

I daydream more as the question and answer session continues.

After class, Wendy gives me a sly look that I can't decipher. What's up with her?

I hope it doesn't have to do with my leaving Jen's house early with Mackie.

Following an uneventful Computer Lab, I rush to the Dining Hall, drop my backpack on a seat at our still-empty table, and stand in line for lunch. When I return, Wes has taken a seat next to mine with Ty sandwiching me on the other side. Mackie, seated across from us, eyes them with a playful smile.

"Hi, Jer," she says quietly, with an innocent look, as I sit down.

I nod back, not sure of what to say.

"Wes just asked how I was feeling," Mackie says, catching me up. "You know, because I left Jen's party early."

Looking away from me and back to Wes, Mackie continues without missing a beat. "I'm feeling much better, thank you. In fact, I'm so much better that I could dance. You know how to dance, right, Wes? You too, Ty?" she asks the questions innocently, looking back and forth between them. Of course she knows they dance. Or, what passes for dancing.

The guys look confused. This is exactly what Mackie has been so good at for years. *Confuse and conquer.* I know her strategy. She isn't going to let Wes push her into talking about why she left Jen's house so early.

Mackie grins at me. By this time, almost all our friends are seated and eating. I look down at my tacos, pick one up, and take a bite.

Mackie waves her arm to get Erica's attention.

"Erica, are you and Jon going to Sadie with anyone?"

Wes and Ty lean in to make sure they hear the conversation. In fact, everyone at our table has settled down, suddenly aware that something is happening. Erica shakes her head, looks at Mackie, and cocks her head to mark the question.

I take another bite of my taco.

"Then, can Jeremy and I catch a ride with you guys?" Mackie's voice sounds like she is setting things up for the four of us to have coffee after school. The way she posed the question sounds so . . . normal.

Giving her a surprised look and then darting a look at me with the same face, Erica squeals, "Oooh, that will be so much fun!" She turns to Jon, seated next to her, as everyone at our table begins buzzing at once.

Mackie looks back at Wes, smiles sweetly, and switches to her faux Southern accent. "Westerly, could I ask you to trade places with me? I'd like to ask Jeremy a little question about our English assignment."

Wes flashes a grin at me and stands up. "Sure, no problem," he says.

Ty's mouth hangs open.

Of course, Jen and Erica get up from their seats and speed over to talk excitedly with Mackie about the dance. When did she ask me? What will she wear? Blah. Blah.

The guys shake their heads at me with accusing looks. I didn't tell them. They've had had to hear it from Mackie.

I smile at Wes. "Angela?" I ask.

He nods, a big grin growing on his face.

While Mackie converses with the girls, Ty endorses me with a thumbs-up.

I chuckle. It's all too crazy. *Yeah, crazy-good!*

After lunch, Mackie and I walk out of the Dining Hall together and head for our English Literature class. The corridor is full of fast-moving people and bouncing noise.

"Are you okay with what I did? I mean about us going with Erica and Jon?" she asks, as we move beyond our friends.

"Oh, yeah. No one even questioned us about leaving Jen's party early. It was all about the dance," I reply.

"But that's not why I asked you. You know that, right?" she asks, concern spilling out of her brown eyes.

"Yeah, I know," I say, and I hope so. Because I know that, besides being very cool and smart, Mackie has another skill. I've watched her over the years. She knows how to set things up to her advantage. Like when she told me to call Jen and make an excuse for our leaving the party. She'd come up with a story to cover our exit with almost no effort. I don't want to believe her asking me to the dance figured into any of that. In fact, I feel lucky to be going with her.

English and French classes over, I walk Mackie downstairs to her locker.

"Will you call me after I finish at the shelter?" she asks.

Nodding, I say goodbye, and hustle to my chemistry class. When class is done, I head to the gym locker room for cross-country practice.

I change into my workout clothes and am putting my shoes on when Brody sits himself next to me on the bench. *Oh, here we go.*

"Tarleton. I hear you're going to Sadie with Mackie. What's that about?"

"She asked me."

"Out of nowhere she just asked you? I don't think so. How long have you two been hanging?" Brody's mouth is a straight, unhappy line in his face. He opens and closes his fists. He looks mean.

"We're not hanging. And if we are? So what?"

"You don't want to go there. You think we're not going to have a problem?"

"According to Mackie, she's not with you. You're with Jilly. Right?" My heart sounds like it's ringing in my ears.

"Don't get cute with me, T-Man," Brody says, his voice ratcheting up in volume as his lips twist. A couple of the guys turn to watch us.

"Look," I say, in as calm a voice as I can manage. "Like I said, she asked me. Why do you care?"

"Because you said you didn't know if she was seeing anyone. You're lying to me, you sack of shit."

"Nothing was going on then. If it had been, I'd have said so, because I don't see how it's a big deal. Or is it? Are you still hung up on her?"

He doesn't answer and stomps off.

I look over at the other guys and shrug.

"If you had any 'nads, you'd punch him," Cole says.

I stare at him. Cole should think about his own gonads.

Out on the track's practice field, Coach has his hands on his hips, kind of rolling them to ease the joints.

He calls out to us, "Come on, come on. Just because we took Riley Park doesn't mean we can lollygag. Does anyone have a problem? No? Good. Listen up. You're doing tempo runs today. Same route as always. I want everyone back here in forty-five minutes. Twenty minutes after four, gentlemen. Now let's go."

I begin running with a loose stride, heading for a nearby island park with trails and woods. The air is cool and dry, more like fall than summer. After my talk with Brody I feel the urge to run hard, but that isn't at all what Coach wants today.

I ease into my warm-up pace, planning to reach peak speed in about twenty minutes. I'll run hard for at least five minutes and slide back down the cycle. For a while, I coast behind Ryan and Cole. Then they increase their pace and disappear around a curve in the trees.

How does Mackie heal animals? I've read about people who train or live with pets and develop an intuitive connection, but never one that involves spontaneous healing.

In the third minute of my peak, a hard shove from behind bounces me off a Doug fir. I land on the ground, on my face.

"Uhhh." My breath pops out of my mouth in a gust.

As I scramble to my feet, Brody moves ahead on the trail. He looks back to make sure I see his smile. My arm burns from where I've hit rough tree bark, and my face feels hot.

I try to catch up with him, wanting to return the shove, but he has the advantage and is too far ahead of me.

How am I going to deal with this? I've wrestled with Jon, Wes, and Ty growing up, but we've never thrown serious punches. Staying away from Mackie isn't an option, though. How can I get Brody off my back? So much for a nice afternoon run.

Back at the practice field, I stretch out and cool down with Ben.

"Great day," he says, smiling up at the sun in a cloudless sky. Being with Ben is settling, something I need as I watch Brody cowboying around with some of the guys.

Coach claps his hands and asks, "Any problems?" He looks us over. "Good, then get dressed and get out of here. Tomorrow we run intervals."

He starts to walk away then turns back. "Our trophy and ribbons should be here Friday. Have a good evening, gentlemen."

Everyone heads back to the locker room. Unable to contain my anger, I approach Brody as we near the building. He acts like nothing is unusual, and keeps walking with Cole. But Cole backs away when he sees the look on my face.

"Why did you do that?" I ask Brody, my voice rough with anger.

"Don't act like you don't know why," he growls. "How long have you been seeing Mackie?"

"She's been my friend for years."

"You lied to me."

"Nothing happened until this weekend when she asked me to the dance. That's two months after she stopped seeing you. What's your problem?"

"Oh, so now you want a piece of her?" he asks.

"Don't talk about her like that."

Brody grabs the front of my shirt.

I snap, pushing back with both my hands on his chest. We end up tangled, on the ground, punching each other.

We fight for maybe fifteen seconds before I hear Coach's voice above us. "Cameron! Tarleton! My office. Now!"

We lay on the ground. My lower left rib and jaw hurt. Brody has hit me hard. I search his face, hoping I've hurt him, too. The pain in my right hand tells me yes. Yes, I have.

"You're a dickhead," Brody hisses at me.

"Brody, shut it," Coach growls. "I sure hope you two can get up, because I'm not going to help you." Then he turns his back on us, and heads into the building.

A few of the guys stand off to the side, watching. Ben walks over and gives me a hand up, his eyes wide as he looks from me to Brody.

I walk ahead of Brody, into Coach's office. The guys are wound up about the fight. I hear Cole say, "If Jeremy had any 'nads . . ."

Coach sits behind his beat-up metal desk in his cinderblock office. He motions for us to be seated in a couple of straight-backed chairs facing the desk. Then he opens the thermos on his desk and pours himself a cup of coffee. He is not smiling.

"So what's this all about?"

Neither of us speaks.

"Okay, tough guys. No talking, no running. That's the deal. Either we settle this now or you're both off the team. What's it going to be?"

"Brody's got a problem because his ex asked me to Sadie One," I grumble.

"Asshole," Brody shoots back.

"I'm not going to warn you another time about your language," Coach says, looking grimly at Brody.

"So, you boys figure the way to resolve this is to duke it out. That's very manly of you. Did you stop to think that would get you kicked off the team? No? Well, then you're not thinking today. Are you?"

He takes another swallow from his cup. "Here's what's going to happen. Sadie One's girls' choice, right? So you're going to let the girl choose. If she wants to go to the dance with Jeremy, then that's the way it is. Brody, you can't decide by yourself that someone's your girlfriend. It's a mutual thing. Got it? Jeremy, I sure hope you know what you're doing because dating the ex of a teammate is a recipe for disaster. But that's up to you."

He flaps a hand in exasperation and takes another sip from his cup.

"If the two of you can't live with this situation then you're no good to this team and you're off. What's it going to be?"

Coach leans back in his chair and looks from Brody to me. His hands shake slightly.

I break the silence first.

"I didn't say yes to Mackie to get to Brody. But I'm going to the dance, and I'll see her for as long as she wants to see me."

"You're a real douche. But you're not worth me losing my letter," Brody responds.

"So is this a truce?" Coach asks. "I want to hear it from both of you. And I want to see a handshake and no more crap out of either of you for the rest of the season. Can you do that?"

I sit up straighter and glance at Brody. "Okay. Unless you come at me first."

Brody looks like he wants to hit me again, immediately, then he relaxes.

"Right," he says. "Mac will get bored. Like tomorrow."

"You're not saying the words I want to hear, Mr. Cameron," Coach says, drumming his fingers on his desk.

Brody stares at Coach like he can't believe he has to say something more, then he grins. "Okay, cool. Let the best man win, you know what I mean. Mac's going to choose me soon enough," he says.

"Shake hands. Now," Coach orders and stands up to show he wants us to be done.

I hold out my hand.

Brody takes it, squeezes very hard, and forces a smile.

Most of the guys have hung around in the locker room to find out what happened.

Cole looks at me and asks, "So?"

"We're still on the team."

Disaster averted. Brody avoids questions by snapping his towel and heading for the showers.

I see Ben, already dressed, lounging on a workout bench.

"Let's go home," I tell him, pulling my clothes out of my locker and stuffing them in my gear bag. I can take a shower at the house.

As we head out the locker room door to the parking lot I say, "Ben. Thanks. For what you did back there."

"*No mas,*" he says, grinning and holding his hands up in mock surrender.

Once home, I trudge upstairs to the bathroom, glad to be by myself. The fight has left me feeling upended and cold, like I might vomit. I look at my face in the mirror, and see a bruise forming where Brody socked my left jaw.

After turning on a small heater in the bathroom to warm the air, I go into my bedroom and pull out a change of clothes and a sweatshirt, then I head into the shower. The hot water eases my tense muscles, but doesn't do much for my racing thoughts. Brody won't just walk away. He'll fester under Coach's no-fight ruling; maybe even make it through part of the season. But I know Brody wants to come after me. And a big part of me wants to do the same thing to him.

After the shower, I rub arnica gel on my jaw and my aching ribs and then slide into my clothes. Hopefully, the gel will reduce the bruising. And the pain.

I hear Mom arrive home from Seattle, and then Justin's feet pounding up the stairs. When Justin is in his room, I move like a snail down the steps, debating whether Mom might have already heard about the fight. Or maybe she's heard from Mrs. Spence about Sadie One.

She might know everything. The island's Moms Network runs deep. My mom knew about the police bust at Spooner's within minutes of Ty texting me. It's hard to do anything without someone's mom or dad knowing about it.

But when I walk gingerly into the kitchen, trying to act like nothing is wrong, Mom just recruits me to help with dinner.

I sit on a bar stool at the counter cutting tomatoes when she notices the bruise on my jaw.

"Where did you get that? At school?" she asks, looking closely at my face.

"Ah, yeah. Brody and I sort of ran into each other. It's nothing."

"How did that happen?"

"Uh, we were fooling around and fell down."

"You boys need to be more careful. You could have broken a tooth. Are you hurt anywhere else?"

"No. I'm okay. Really."

Dad comes in, sniffs the air, and raises his eyebrows at Mom.

"Chicken and noodle casserole," Mom says.

"Mmmm. So how are things going here?" Dad asks her, patting her arm.

"I was looking at a bruise that Jeremy has near his mouth. He and Brody got a little wild at school today," Mom replies. I was hoping not to have to go over this with Dad.

Dad waits for me to speak.

"We, ah, fell down," I explain.

"People don't just spontaneously fall down," Dad says. When I don't respond he says, "Jeremy, take some time to think about what happened and how it could have been avoided." He doesn't understand. It will get worse if I let Brody push me around.

I finish the salad, set it on the table, and return to my room. The casserole will take more time to warm before it's ready to eat, and I want to talk with Mackie. She should be home from the shelter. Stretching out on my bed, I send:

can U talk

She replies:

Dinner now. Later?

My reply:

sure

Justin eases into my room and waits next to my desk.

"What's up?" I ask.

"You are cordially invited to dine with the family," Justin announces in a formal voice, bowing low. He definitely is watching too many old movies.

"Okay, I'll be down," I reply, and slip my phone into my pants pocket after he leaves the room. I don't want Justin to see how much it hurts me to get up. He would have questions. Maybe even ask them in front of Mom and Dad.

I am seated at the table with my mouth full of casserole when Mom turns to me.

"Jeremy, is there anything else you want to tell us?"

Seeing her face, I know that she isn't referring to the fight. She looks way too happy.

"Ah, Mackie asked me to Sadie One," I say, spearing some salad with a fork.

"You're going to Sadie with Mackie! That's wonderful! When did she ask you?" Mom can barely contain herself.

Oh, this could be a problem. Mackie asked me to the dance three days ago, and I didn't mention anything to them.

"Not long ago," I reply.

Dad and Justin look at me like I have some explaining to do. Sadie One isn't computing for them.

Mom beats me to it, speaking fast. "You remember this from last year, right? Jeremy went to Sadie Two. Sadie One is the first of two fall dances. Each dance has music from a decade in the last century. Sadie One is fifties music. After Sadie, the boys ask the girls to Steve One. That will be a sixties dance. Jeremy, I could show you some steps," she offers.

"Uh, the Dance Club puts on a clinic the first half hour. I think I'll be okay."

I don't want her too into this. That would mean one full week of more attention than I can handle. She really bugged me last spring when Cat Morley asked me to the Sadie Two disco dance, and I don't want a repeat of her trying to get me enthused about dancing.

"You know, I thought Mackie was dating Brody. What happened there?" Mom asks, frowning.

"Don't know," I say. "She stopped seeing him after the accident."

"So does that bruise have anything to do with you going with Mackie to the dance?"

"He seemed a little ticked off," I say, hoping it would be enough.

"You were in a fight today over Mackie?"

"He thinks she's still into him, even though he's seeing Jilly Parker now."

"Did you get in trouble?"

"Coach told us to knock it off."

This gets Dad's attention. "Are you on probation?" he asks.

"No. Coach made us promise to leave each other alone. So I guess it's over," I say then fill my mouth with casserole.

" 'I guess it's over?' " Mom asks, in her college instructor's voice.

I take a while to swallow. "Yeah, I guess it's over."

"Fighting isn't like you, Jeremy. What happened?" Mom continues.

"No blood was spilled. Coach didn't kick us off the team. Can I just finish dinner?" This comes out sounding whiny, not the best way to get my mom off the subject.

Mom and Dad exchange 'The Look' that I've never been able to decode. It seems to end the discussion, though, because they don't ask more questions.

After dinner I put my plate in the dishwasher and slowly walk upstairs to finish my homework.

Fifteen minutes later, my phone buzzes. It's Mackie.

"Hi," she says. "I heard about the fight. Are you okay?"

I feel a lot better hearing her voice.

"Yeah, I'm fine. It wasn't bad. Coach stopped us before anything really happened."

"I should have known Brody would go after you. This is my fault. I'm sorry."

"Don't be sorry. It wasn't your fault. Brody has a short fuse. Hey, what happened at the shelter today?"

"Some people were out on Locke's Pass and saw an eagle lying on the north shore. They called it in. Gabe drove over to pick him up, and I rode along. Gabe said he was cut like he'd been in a fight with another eagle."

"What happened when the bird saw you?"

"Not much, because he was so bad off. At first Gabe thought he was stunned or playing dead, but his wounds are serious. We brought him back to the shelter, and Gabe logged him as Number 27. He's by himself in one of the recovery cages. Tomorrow I'll try to spend time with him."

"Wow," I say, wishing I could have been there, too. "What did Number 26 do?"

"She was up and flying. She called out a few times. He tried to answer. Gabe said they had probably figured out some things about each other."

"Probably a lot," I say. "At least each other's sex and age. Did she get a look at him?"

"I don't know."

"How old is he?"

"He's young, still a juvenile."

"Where's he injured?"

"He can't extend one of his wings, and his feet and the top of his head were covered in blood."

"Oh, yeah. Definitely a fight," I say, thinking that I was lucky today with Brody compared to Number 27's fight.

"So, it's serious," I say.

"Yeah. Doc came right away."

"Hmmm. When you were on your way to find him, did you feel the same kind of connection that you had with the orca?"

"It's always the same, but a little different, too. It wasn't strong today. He was in shock and couldn't even look at me. And I don't feel tired like I was after the orca. Maybe how large the animal is makes a difference."

This is something that hadn't occurred to me.

"So, what did you feel today?"

"I was being pulled, but not like with the orca. Not even close. Still, when we were at the shelter, it was hard to leave him."

"What does that mean?"

She's quiet for a few seconds.

"Remember when I told you the orca pulled me along and I felt like I was in a vacuum? I have that same feeling with other animals. It always seems like I'm pulled through an air stream before I make contact with them."

According to everything I know about science and animals, consistent commonalities have significance. Feeling pulled along like she is in a vacuum has something to do with every incident. And only Mackie can feel it. I've never felt anything like that at the shelter by myself, when Mackie and I have worked together, or when we were with the orca.

She interrupts my thoughts.

"I feel really bad about this thing with you and Brody. Where did he hit you?"

"It's nothing. Don't worry."

"I'm worried."

I'm not thinking about Brody. I care about Mackie. Will she ever tell me everything about this connection she has with animals? But I have homework. Reluctantly, I say good night and hang up. My jaw aches from Brody's fist.

Chapter 6

Mackie sits next to me every day at lunch, and we walk to our afternoon classes together. I can't seem to get enough of being with her. *Does she feel the same way about me?*

Wednesday, as we leave the Dining Hall, she says, "Doc was in yesterday. He told us Number 27's wounds are healing. Did you know that eagles have a high rate for infection after being in a fight?"

"Yeah, we've had other eagles brought in that ended up being really sick. Two didn't make it. Can you tell whether he's getting better because of you? Like how you knew that the whale was better?" I ask.

"Yes. But it's different with Number 27 than it was with the whale. I think the orca knew what was happening. That I could help him. With Number 27, I need to wait for him to connect. It might be all the sedatives." She pauses, and sighs. "But he's going to be fine."

After dinner, I run to Mackie's house and we translate our French assignment. Noelle checks us out as we sit together on the couch, but leaves us alone. *Maybe Mackie said something to her?*

Actually, it has been a great week in many ways. Brody has calmed down, and hasn't bothered me at practice. Or, maybe he's just ignoring me. That's just fine. I've always thought of cross-country as my second favorite sport after soccer, but now, running distance feels great. Tuesday, we had interval training on the track, 600s broken up by 200s. Then, even with Brody running next to me, Wednesday's practice went well. The team ran for about forty minutes, followed by a coaching clinic.

Now it's Thursday and Coach holds his hand up to give us instructions in the locker room. "Gentlemen, today we run a fartlek." Like always, there are a few snickers. Coach doesn't look amused. "Remember, at the end of every quarter mile you run a fifteen second sprint. Use the wooded trail route, and follow our markers. No cheating. I want to see every one of you breathing hard when you get back here. Forty minutes." He looks at his watch. "Starting now." Coach holds the door open as we sweep out into the bright sunshine.

I begin running at an easy pace, thinking how much more interesting my life has become. Mackie is definitely the reason. Thirty minutes in, I hear footsteps pounding up fast behind me. It's Ben, grinning like a madman. He tries to pass me and we mock-race each other back to school. Later, I feel so tired I fall asleep before my head hits my pillow.

On Friday, Erica sits next to me during lunch while I wait for Mackie and says, "Mackie's really excited about the dance."

I feel my heartbeat pick up.

"Yeah, well, I am the Dance Master," I tell her, making an effort to look casual, but serious.

She crosses her eyes at me, and we both laugh.

"Yeah, I'm happy she asked me to the dance," I add.

Of course there's more to it. The thing I like most about being with Mackie is that when we're alone she likes to hold hands, kiss, and cuddle. But, at school or with our friends, she's cool. There isn't any big show. Some girls get all over guys. Not Mackie. She might put a little flirt on, but she doesn't do anything just to get attention.

Because it's Friday we don't have practice, so there's plenty of time after school to kick back at the house before Jon and Erica pick me up for Sadie One. I've been looking forward to it because, though I'm not the world's greatest dancer, Mackie picked me to go with her. That's enough.

After dinner I change into pretty much what I might wear for school: a pair of dark jeans and an olive-green and black plaid shirt left unbuttoned over a red T-shirt. I'll carry my rain jacket because the air has a heaviness that promises a change of weather.

As I jog back downstairs, Mom stands in the front door hallway. She raises her fists in her mom's victory salute when she sees me. "Jeremy you look so nice. Those colors are perfect on you," she nods, giving me a quick hug.

"I don't have anything that looks fifties. It's okay, I guess."

"Nolan," Mom calls to Dad, who is in the front room, "Jeremy's leaving."

Dad walks out with Justin, who stares like he's trying to figure out what all the fuss is about.

"Ah, who's driving tonight?" Dad asks. I've gone over this with Mom, but not Dad. He and Justin have been playing chess, their game most Friday nights.

"Jon. We'll be with Erica and Jon. After the dance we're going to Mackie's. Wes and Angela, too. Mr. and Mrs. Spence know about it."

"All right. Call us if something happens and you need a ride," Dad says, turning. He wants to get back to the game board.

"Two more things," Mom says as I head toward the vestibule door to wait on the porch. "You probably won't think this is important, but I bought a silk flower on campus for you to give to Mackie." She holds out a lavender flower with a dusting of gold glitter in the middle. "She can wear this in her hair. See, it has a clip. Also, you don't have to be back until midnight, or whenever Caitlin and Nick decide it's time for you kids to go home. I hope you have a lot of fun."

I hug her.

"Thanks, Mom," I say, handling the flower carefully. "I mean it, thanks. I didn't know I was supposed to get her something."

"Well, now you know. If she doesn't want to wear it, that's not a problem. It's the thought of the gift that counts."

Right. I need to start thinking more.

At seven-fifteen, Jon and Erica pull down our driveway. I leap off the front porch steps to meet them. The dance is scheduled from seven thirty to ten o'clock and we still have to pick Mackie up.

Erica greets me first. "Hey Jer, are you ready to twist and shout?" she asks, flipping her twin pigtails back and forth.

"Isn't that from the sixties?" I reply, opening the back door of Jon's vintage Volkswagen Jetta.

"Oh poo!" Erica mutters. "Who cares? It's going to be jumping and jiving tonight," she sings.

"This is what I've had to deal with today," Jon says, as he puts the car in drive and we quickly cross the distance to Mackie's house. But I know Jon. He's totally crushing on Erica. Maybe that's how I act around Mackie, too.

As Jon and Erica wait, I climb out of the car and walk to the Spences' front door. Two weeks ago, I would have waited with Jon and Erica for Mackie to come out. Now things are different. When I tap the doorknocker, Mac opens the door right away. I smile big.

Mackie is beautiful! She has on a tan, black, and ivory leopard print sweater with a small pearl necklace, and tight black jeans that made her legs look really long. Her hair is pulled in a high ponytail at the back of her head. It makes her doe-like eyes look even bigger. Mac's mom and dad watch us just behind her. Noelle prances at their side.

"Hello, Jeremy. Oh, that's lovely," Mrs. Spence says as I silently hand Mackie the lavender flower.

"Hi, Mrs. Spence, Mr. Spence," I reply, smiling at them and trying to avoid looking at Noelle. I do not want to trigger a Suffering Southern Belle scene.

"Mackie, my mom found this flower on campus for me to give to you. You can put it in your hair if you want," I explain, trying to sound like I know what I'm talking about.

"Thank you! It's like a fairytale flower," Mackie says. Mrs. Spence motions for me to step inside as Mackie leaves the room with the flower.

Meanwhile, Noelle eyes me like she might have something to say. I try not to make contact with her. It's tough, though, avoiding the extraterrestrial in the room.

Mackie returns, and I notice she's added the flower to the top of her ponytail. The sparkles glitter against her dark hair.

Then, with her parents calling after us, "Have fun!" we walk out the front door, and join Jon and Erica in the car. Erica has moved to the back seat to talk with Mackie. My legs thank her.

"Ooh, I like your hair!" Erica says.

"Jeremy gave me this flower," Mackie replies, touching the back of her ponytail and giving me more credit than I deserve.

"Jon gave me a wrist corsage, but I was afraid it would get crushed when we dance, so I put it in some water at home," Erica says.

I look at Jon, and we both roll our eyes at their girl talk. But we listen.

At school, we cram our jackets and shoes into Jon's locker, since it's the closest to the gym. Mom told me this kind of dance was dubbed a "Sock Hop" because in the 1950s, wooden gym floors weren't varnished. They damaged easily, so everyone danced without shoes, in their socks. We will do the same to carry on the tradition.

Entering the gym, I'm shocked to see so many people. This is a much bigger dance than last year's Sadie Two disco dance. The Dance Club is already demonstrating steps, so we find places to sit on an upper bleacher.

The music is DJ'ed and loud. In between songs, Mr. McDowell, the Dance Club's faculty advisor, explains the dance steps. They don't look that difficult, and I begin looking around to see who else is in the stands. I catch sight of Wes and Angela sitting with some other juniors near us. Wes sees me and waves.

Mackie links her arm in mine and we rock in our seats with the music. After about fifteen minutes of instruction, the Dance Club invites everyone onto the floor. We stand up at once and head down the steps, the sound muffled by the socks on our feet.

"Get ready to rock 'n' roll, because we have 'Rock Around the Clock' by Bill Haley and the Comets, 'Peggy Sue' by Buddy Holly, and 'At the Hop' by Danny and the Juniors," Mr. McDowell announces.

When the music starts, the beat comes fast. Most people just free style. So do I, and have to keep myself from knocking into people dancing around me. After a while I don't worry too much, because it's impossible. People keep bumping into me. But I try to keep Mackie safe.

"Jer, just do what I do, but in reverse," Mac suggests after we mash out some steps that aren't even close to being together. "Left foot, then step again with your left foot. Now your right foot, then step again with your right foot. Then go backwards with your left foot. That's it!"

"Right," I say, not sure of much of anything.

Mackie gasps in surprise when I spin her under my arm.

"You've been practicing!" She smiles.

What practicing? I try to look mysterious. But Mackie looks happy and that's what matters. That, and the handholding.

At the end of the third song, Mr. McDowell picks up the mic again.

"Now it's time for a line dance. The Dance Club showed you this earlier. Please form two lines about six feet apart and, when you finish, stay at the end of the line and the next dancer will dance down, and so on. Okay, ready to go? This song is called 'The Stroll' by the Diamonds."

Mackie and I face each other with Jon and Erica and six people I don't know. The beat is slow, like you could actually walk to the music. Those who can't, dance free style, so I don't feel too weird when it's my turn. But most of the girls and two of the guys in our line can really dance. Mackie walks between our two lines with her eyes half closed, syncing to the music and snapping her fingers. The rest of the room may as well be empty. She is all I see.

After the line dance there are three more fast songs and then it's time for another workshop from the Dance Club, who demonstrate 1950s slow dance steps.

"Jer, let's try this," Mackie urges.

"Okay. Just know that I'm sorry when I step on your feet."

Mackie sends me a terrified look and we both laugh as we begin dancing 1-2-3-4, making a box with our feet. Holding Mackie's hand and guiding her with my other hand on her waist is new for me. And she rests her left hand on my shoulder. We'd never danced together like that before.

After the workshop, 'Come with Me' by the Del-Vikings plays. Sure, the song has sappy lyrics, but that doesn't matter. I breathe in the vanilla-orange of Mackie's hair, and she moves with me like we've danced together forever. Somehow, I avoid stepping all over her feet.

I twirl her a couple of times, slowly, watching as her eyes light up, and she wriggles her hips. Then she tries to twirl me. That cracks us up, and we dance the last steps laughing.

Right after the tune ends, Mr. McDowell announces three fast songs. The only one I know is 'Kansas City' by Wilbert Harrison, a blues-rock classic covered by lots of bands. It's definitely a crowd pleaser. Just about everyone gets on the floor to jam.

Halfway through Sadie One, we have a fifteen-minute break in dancing. As music continues to play on the sound system, Mackie and I see a wave of our friends led by Wes, Angela, Jon, and Erica.

The girls want to use the restroom, which means they'll be gone for all of the fifteen minutes. So I head with the guys to the end of the gym where tables are topped by soft drinks and fruit-flavored sparkling water. My throat and lips feel dry. Not as bad as when I run, but close. Red, blue, and black 1950s toy cars, big sets of dice, and a flowered tablecloth decorate the beverage table. Pink, green, and gold Japanese paper lanterns twirl slowly under the overhead lights.

Jilly stands nearby with a pack of sophomores. She doesn't look happy and keeps searching around the big room. I don't see Brody.

"Jeremy," Wes jolts me out from my fog. "You and Mac look good out there. What's up with that?" he teases me.

"Oh, she's okay," I say. The guys look at me like I've gone mental. Then I smile and slap my forehead. "Dancing with Mackie is . . . better than just about anything."

"Nice," Wes agrees, nodding in approval.

Near the end of the break, Erica and Angela sock-skate back to us. *Where is Mackie?* Erica sees the question on my face and aims directly for me, getting so close I can hear her breathing.

"Brody's with Mackie. He looks kind of wild," she blurts.

"Where?" I ask, my body tensing.

"By the Chem labs." Erica looks like she will go for Mackie if I don't.

I try to get out of the room as fast as I can, pushing against the crowd returning to the gym. What is going on between Brody and Mackie?

Once I clear the double doors, I dodge a group of girls and sprint down a side hallway. There, under long panels of dimmed overhead lighting, I see them. Brody's hands are on the wall behind Mackie as he leans in. Mackie catches my movement out of the corner of her eye and holds up a hand for me to stop.

I don't. When I'm ten paces from them she says, "Give us a minute, Jer. I want to make sure Brody and I are clear about something."

She says it so charmingly, and with a shake of her head like this is just another time she has to make something plain to that silly Brody. I wonder if she might really have things under control.

Then Brody leans in closer. I'm not going anywhere.

"I'd rethink that, Brody," I growl.

He turns to look at me like I'm just coming into focus for him.

"We're done when I say we are," he says to me, or maybe to Mackie. Then he stands up straight, and steps away from her with a shitty grin.

"Think about what I said," Mackie says to him.

Brody shrugs. "This isn't over."

"Don't think I won't do it," Mackie counters.

What is going on? What does Mackie mean?

Brody turns, sneers at me, and stomps off. Mackie falls back against the wall and closes her eyes.

In a second I'm next to her. She starts to shake.

"Are you okay?" I ask.

"Yeah. Jeremy, I don't want you to go after Brody. He's my problem, and I need to handle it. I'm serious. It would kill me if he hurt you again, because of me. Let's go back to the gym. I'll tell you what happened, but right now I just want to get out of here."

She looks rattled.

I put my arm around her waist and she does the same with me. We walk back to the dance. A fast song is playing, but I don't feel like dancing. I lead Mackie to the closest stand of bleachers. We climb up to the third row and sit.

Mackie hugs her knees with her arms, looks out into the crowd of dancers, and takes a big breath. "It's like he's obsessed," she says. "I told him if he doesn't leave me alone, I'll go to his parents. His mother knows I wouldn't make this up." She pauses and bites her lower lip. Then she turns her eyes to mine. "I told him his fight is with me, not you," she says.

I hold her hand in mine. "I'm not going to let him do anything that you don't want. But what did the two of you do? I mean, what were you to each other?" I've asked the questions knowing I might not like the answers.

She gives me a startled look and then a slight smile.

"There's not much to tell you. I know everyone thinks that since Brody and I were together, we were doing it." She grimaces. "It was never that way. I never liked him that way. But I've been trying to figure out this odd feeling I have when he's around. Don't take this wrong. It's just that I seem to know what Brody's going to do, and he seems to know what I'm going to do whenever we're around each other."

She's never liked him!

"I think he views me as a challenge." She waves her hands like it seems preposterous to her too. "He wanted to see me a lot more than I wanted to see him. This summer, after the accident, I told him to forget it. And me. But he still texts and calls all the time."

"That's it? What does he want?" I ask, astonished by what I've heard. Mackie has shut Brody out? The guy has a reputation as a big-time player with the ladies in our school.

"He acts like I owe him something and now he's ready to collect. I think he actually believes it," she says, shaking her head.

I take her hand again and smile reassuringly.

"Do you want to stay?" I ask.

She doesn't say anything, just stands up, steps slowly down the bleacher stairs, turns, and looks up at me with both hands outstretched.

'Sea of Love' is playing and she feels warm and soft as we slow dance. This time, I hold her close. Against-school-rules close. I hope the song will never end.

When Sadie One is over, everyone clears the gym, fast. We meet Jon and Erica at Jon's locker, retrieve our shoes and jackets, and walk in the cool, damp air to his car. Jon and Erica, in the two front seats, excitedly review the dance and don't seem to notice Mackie's and my silence.

When we arrive at the Spences' house, Wes and Angela are in his car bobbing to music, waiting for us. Mackie seems to get a second wind as we head to the front door.

Inside, Mr. and Mrs. Spence greet us, ask about the dance, and offer fresh popcorn. As the adults retreat, we stampede to the kitchen. I watch for Noelle, but she never shows up.

Erica asks, "Mackie, do you still have your Ouija board?"

The girls giggle. I know from previous experience what's coming.

When we were kids, Mackie told us the Ouija board belonged to her great-great-aunt, a spiritual medium who lived in Atlanta during the 1930s. Shunned by her church for her "black magic," Martha Spence had made a very good living on the Eastern seaboard, using the board to hold séances for wealthy women who became her clients.

Mackie opens a large cabinet in the great room that houses electronic and board games. She returns with a flat, antique wooden box whose colorful printed image has faded with time.

Opening the hinged top, she carefully sets the playing board on the dining room table and the six of us ring the table, taking seats. Lifting out the planchette, a small heart-shaped piece of wood, and placing this indicator in the middle of the playing board, Mackie looks up to make sure the game is what everyone still wants to do.

She dims the lights and places a candle on the table. Mac told us years ago that candlelight improves Ouija board outcomes. I've wondered if the low light covers up some kind of visual trick.

"Angela, do you know how to play?" Mackie asks as she lights the candle.

"No, this is all new to me," Angela says.

"Just watch. It's easy. You ask someone a question. They place their fingers on this planchette piece that always starts out in the middle of the board. Supposedly a spirit guides your answer to point the planchette to letters or numbers," Mackie explains.

Erica raises her hand.

"Jon," she says, I have a question for you. Are you ready?"

He squints at her and wrinkles his nose, but places his fingertips on the planchette.

"Okay, let's do this, but you have to play FireStorm," he says, negotiating for time with Erica on another game.

Erica grins and nods at him.

"Who do you like?" Erica asks.

Jon snaps his neck back and forth, and makes gurgling noises like he is possessed. The pointer moves first to a *J*, then an *E*, next a *T*, and then drifts away and returns to the *T* and then an *A*. *JETTA*. Jon likes his car, a hand-me-down Volkswagen Jetta.

Everyone breaks up laughing. So far, the Ouija spirit is 0 for one.

Jon celebrates with an arm-pump, points a finger at Erica, and gloats, "You owe me a FireStorm. Prepare to burn."

Erica takes it all in good humor. She and Jon are, after all, evenly matched gamers.

"Now you go, Wes," Erica says. "Angela, ask him something."

Angela puts her hands up and fans them back and forth, as if to say no-no. But once the Ouija board questioning starts, no one can get away with saying they don't want to play.

Angela pauses for a moment then grins and says, "I'm going to ask a simple question. Wes, what are you doing this weekend?"

Looking very serious, Wes places his fingers lightly on the planchette and makes an eerie sound, "Oooo." The response on the board is *JAVA WITH ANGELA*. Angela looks thrilled with his answer and blushes. She's kind of cute.

Then Erica turns to me. "Jeremy, it's your turn. Ask a question."

Looking at Mackie, I hesitate. I don't want to ask anything that will cause her more stress after tonight's episode with Brody.

"Mackie, what's in your future?" She can go anywhere with that.

Mackie shoots me a quick smile, inclines her head so that she looks like she is really concentrating, and begins. *D, A, N, G, E,* and resists adding *R*.

"Danger!" Erica shrieks. "What do you mean? You have to give us more!"

Mackie looks shocked. She glances at me across the table, then slides her eyes away from mine and puts her fingertips back on the planchette. She picks out letters that read *DARK WATER*. No one makes a sound. Is this about what Mackie went through in June, when she nearly drowned?

Mackie recovers first, and says, "Those words are in the past. This Ouija is way too old. Jeremy, it's my turn to ask you something."

The remote look I'd seen in her eyes has too swiftly been replaced with mischief.

As I shift so that I can put my fingers on the planchette, she locks her eyes on mine.

"Jeremy, what's in your future?" she asks, repeating my question to her. I feel the token slide under my fingers, and have to wonder why it always feels like there's a magnet under the board. My mind is blank. Unlike Jon and Wes, I'm not going to try to be funny. I spell *SAVE AKESO*.

I look up quickly and say, "Huh, weird. It doesn't mean anything to me. Does anyone know the word Akeso? Who wants to play cards? Texas Hold 'Em?" It hasn't escaped me, though, that Mackie has the same stunned look on her face as when she chose her own letters.

"Yeah, poker. We need a real game," Wes stresses in a voice far deeper than normal.

Everyone gets up. Some go to the kitchen for more snacks. Mackie returns the game board to the cabinet and places two well-worn decks of cards on the table. It's just after eleven, so we have plenty of time for a few rounds. I think about her expression when she saw what I'd spelled out. She'd been surprised and closed her eyes. *Interesting.* What is her interpretation of "Save Akeso," "danger," and "dark water"? What do those words mean?

Before the card game begins, I expect Mackie to whisper something about our Ouija board answers in my ear. She never says a word.

At a quarter to midnight, Mr. Spence walks into the room. "Anybody need a ride home?" he asks.

That's his way of saying that the party is over.

I tell Jon that I'll walk home, even though it has started to rain. Mackie and I stand on the front porch and wave goodbye to our friends. I want to ask her about our Ouija responses, but her eyes are half closed, and she looks like she could fall asleep on her feet. I feel tired, too.

"Jeremy, thank you for going to the d . . . ," she starts to say, but I stop her with a kiss. She hugs me to her, and Mackie is stronger than she looks, so it's a really big hug.

"The dance was special because I was there with you," she says.

Somehow I find my voice. "Yeah. I really had a good time, too. I hope your feet survived the night."

She laughs.

"Maybe tomorrow we can walk in early to the shelter?" she asks.

I nod, and we say goodnight.

I watch as she turns and goes back in the house, then I turn on my flashlight and plunge into the rain-cooled, deep night. In no time I'm home and in bed, dreaming of dancing with Mackie, dark water swirling at our feet.

CHAPTER 7

I sleep in Saturday morning past nine, and wake with images of Mackie, the dance, and dark water still in my head. I want to call her, but decide the memory of us dancing will have to do because I don't want her to think I'm pushy, like Brody.

Throwing the covers off, my muscles tense as I move from warm to cool air. Mom and Dad won't turn the heat on until mid-October. It costs a lot to heat our house, so we just tough out cold, late summer mornings. I climb into a pair of old warm-up pants and pull a heavy sweater over my T-shirt. Then I put on a pair of thick socks. Pushing under the covers again to stay warm, I recall the two words I pieced together on the Ouija board: *SAVE AKESO*.

I prop myself up against my headboard, and reach over to my desk for my notebook. After tapping in 'save akeso' I expect no response from my browser. But oh yeah, the fish are biting!

Akeso: A Greek goddess of the healing process. One of several children of Asclepius, the god of healing and medicine, and his wife Epione. Akeso and her sisters, Hygieia and Panaceia, are linked to health. Akeso (also called Aceso) specifically represents the process of curing wounds and illness. Akeso is derived from the Greek word akesis, meaning healing or curing.

I try to add it up: Hurt or sick animals improve when Mackie is with them. A whale pulled her to him, and she made him better. Akeso can't be a name I came up with by chance last night.

But Mackie aids wounded animals. Had Akeso healed animals too, like Mackie? Is there even a connection?

Better question: What does Mackie know? Her reaction when I spelled 'SAVE AKESO' on the Ouija board was shock. The words clearly meant something to her.

Now totally awake, I have to share this with Mackie before we walk to the shelter. I send her a message:

i found something can U meet? when?

Within about a minute her reply comes in:

Now is good. UR house?

It's after ten. Mom teaches a Saturday morning class, and Dad and Justin usually spend Saturday time together in Dad's office above the garage. I walk out of my room, onto the stairway landing, and listen. It's quiet, so they've already left. Mackie and I should have privacy. I send another message:

11:00 is good C U soon

I head downstairs to the kitchen and pop a slice of bread in our toaster. Spreading peanut butter and blackberry jam on the toast, I eat fast, finishing with a sliced orange.

After returning upstairs, I take a quick shower and dress in jeans and a long-sleeved T-shirt. Then I carry my notebook downstairs to the family room and set it on a low table in front of the couch. Either Mom or Dad started a fire last night in our wood stove. The pressed logs still burn, and the air in the room feels toasty.

I watch Mackie through the front window as she walks down our driveway. She doesn't look any different than any other day. Her hair swings behind her back, and she wears a zipped-up warm-up jacket. My heart starts pumping faster.

I hurry to meet her at the front door.

"Hi," I say. "I found something."

Mackie doesn't say anything, just sends me a questioning look. She follows me into our family room.

"This may be a clue about what's been happening. Remember that word I spelled out on the Ouija board last night? Akeso. Take a look at this," I say, pointing to my notebook.

We sit together on the couch. Mackie leans in to read what I have pulled up on the screen, her hair swinging forward so I can't see her expression. When she finishes and sits back, she looks puzzled. I'm disappointed; I'd hoped for more of a reaction.

"What do you think this means?" she asks, resting back on the cushions and keeping her eyes on mine.

"Well, I think it has to be related to what's happening. I'd never heard of Akeso or her family before reading about them today."

She looks doubtful.

"I know it's weird but follow me on this. Animals heal faster when you're around and somehow, all of a sudden, the name Akeso pops up on the Ouija when I'm thinking about you. Akeso is a healer. Is there a connection?" I stop. I want her to tell me what it means.

Mackie's eyes no longer hold mine. She seems to be off somewhere in her head. For a minute we're both quiet, as she rereads what is on the screen.

"Does this mean anything to you?" she asks in a soft voice. *She looks sorry for me. Why does she feel sorry for me?*

"You're able to heal animals. We don't have anything in animal science to explain it. What if it's a different kind of explanation?"

"You mean a mythological explanation?" she asks.

"Ah, let's not go that far. Do you know where your ancestors came from?"

"My great-great-grandparents came from Scotland and Ireland. Before that, I don't know," she says thoughtfully, twisting a piece of her hair in her fingers, something I've watched her do since we were little when she's trying to figure things out.

"Okay, I know about the human genome and how everyone is related, but will you ask your mom and dad specifically if any of your ancestors came from Greece or Italy?"

"If they did, so what? It doesn't prove anything," she replies with a shrug.

"It could be a clue," I return, unwilling to give up. This is the first break we've had, and we should follow it through. It feels like she's not telling me everything.

"Jeremy," she grins suddenly. "If I'm a goddess, you have to obey me."

I roll my eyes at her.

"Right." I snort. "You already pretty much get whatever you want."

"Oh, but I could ask for so much more," she says, mischief all over her face now. I reach over, run my hands through her hair, and pretend-wrestle her in a hug.

Laughing, she hugs me back then sits up.

"Really, Mackie. You'd tell me if this means something, right? You know I won't talk about this with anyone else. It's cool if you're a goddess," I tease her.

Her laughing eyes become serious.

"I'll ask whether we have any relatives from the Mediterranean," she says and stands. "Do you still want to walk to the shelter together?"

"If I say no, you might turn me into dust!"

She giggles, her eyes closing down to slits, and then she leaves, walking quickly up the driveway and out of sight.

I climb the stairs back to my room, holding tight to my notebook, and try to read my history assignment and review for our chemistry test. My attention isn't good. I'll be lucky if I remember half of the words in front of me. Images from the last twenty-four hours keep popping up in my brain.

Mackie couldn't give me a direct response to my question about whether any of her ancestors came from Greece or Italy. They could represent a genetic linkage. But there are other reasons why I have trouble focusing on my homework. I think about how soft and smooth Mackie's hair is, and how it felt to hold her when we danced last night. And today, when I hugged her on the couch.

A month ago, I'd never spend this much time thinking about any girl. But Mackie isn't just any girl. She trusts me, confides in me, and I'll protect whatever her secret is. Because I know she has a secret. It definitely has to do with her ability to heal animals, and maybe something to do with her gene pool.

My phone buzzes with a new text. Wes:

Want 2 go 2 Cisco's 2nite? What about Mac? Ty, Jon & Erica R in.

Our group likes Cisco's, an all-ages club in Seattle eight blocks from the ferry dock. We went there for the first time two years ago, when an island band, Low Hanging Fruit, played in a contest. Wes knew the bassist, Lars, and Lars was cool. The band didn't win, but we had a great time.

Since then we'd gone to Cisco's every few months. At first it was just the guys, but as of last summer the girls had come with us, too.

I speed downstairs and outside to ask Dad if I can go. As I enter the garage, I listen for sounds from his office loft. Dad always plays background music when he works. Electronic keyboard sounds fill the building, so I know he is upstairs.

"Dad," I call out. "Can I ask you a question?"

No response. I climb the stairs. Justin and Dad sit opposite each other, facing into their screens, deep in computer space. Dad's working, while Justin gestures at his screen like he always does when playing a game by himself.

"Hello?" I say to the air.

Still no response. I walk further in, to the side of Dad's desk.

"Jeremy. What's up?" Dad asks when he catches sight of me.

"Wes, Ty, Jon, and Erica are going to Cisco's tonight. Okay if I go, too?"

"It's fine with me. But Mom will be home soon. You'll have to check with her. I think we may take Justin to see a movie tonight. Something about King Arthur. If you don't go to Seattle, you're welcome to come with us."

"Uh, okay. Thanks. I'll wait for Mom," I say, and retreat down the stairs.

Back in the house, I head for the kitchen. I didn't have much for breakfast and yogurt sounds good. Mom will be home soon, but on Saturdays she doesn't make lunch for us. Any animal will eat based on ease of access. I'm no different; I'll eat anything in the refrigerator. After a cup of yogurt, I microwave a hot dog. I'm just finishing when Mom opens the back porch door and enters the kitchen. She dumps an armload of stuff from school on the chair nearest the door.

"Oh, Jeremy, whatever you're having smells so good. A hot dog? Would you please put one in for me? I haven't had anything since I left this morning. Thank you, dear," she says. Mom is a fine, opportunistic animal. Just like me.

"How was the dance?" she asks as she moves her laptop and a plastic bag of school stuff to the table.

"Great! Mackie knew how to do some of the steps, so that helped. Then we went to her house and played cards. Oh, yeah, she really liked the flower a lot. She put it in her hair." I hope the description is enough to satisfy Mom. It isn't.

"C'mon, I want details. What did the gym look like? What were the girls wearing? Do you remember any of the songs?" she asks.

We sit at the kitchen table as she eats, and I recount, as best as I can, how everything looked. I tell her about the overhead Japanese umbrellas and the toy cars on the tables.

"The Dance Club's costumes were awful. Almost as bad as Sadie Two last year. I thought bellbottoms were ugly, but pictures of poodle dogs on skirts are just weird. Did people really think those were cool back then?"

Mom chuckles. "Probably. Be careful. Someday, kids might say the same thing about what you're wearing."

"No!"

But she looks happy, like she can see the entire dance. Of course, I've left out the parts about Brody's weirdness and our Ouija board results.

"Honey, dances are only going to get better for you," Mom says.

"Hey," I say, "is it okay if I go to Cisco's tonight with the guys? Erica's coming with us. Maybe Mackie. Dad says it's fine with him."

"How are you getting to the ferry?"

"Wes."

"Wes is just driving to the ferry, not in Seattle, right? You're going on as walk ons? And you'll be back by eleven thirty?"

"Yeah, sure. The first set's at eight so we'll make the ten forty-five boat home. I might be a few minutes late if we drop Ty and Mackie off first," I say.

Mom adds mustard and relish to her hot dog. "Who's playing tonight?"

"Don't know. Some band Wes likes."

"What are Justin and Dad doing?"

"The usual," I say. Mom and I have had this conversation so many Saturdays that she knows what I mean.

"What time are we eating tonight?" I asked.

"Early, around five o'clock. We're taking Justin to a movie that starts at six-fifteen, so we'll leave before six. What time will Wes pick you up?"

"Don't know. I think we need to be on the seven-ten boat."

I retreat to the refrigerator to find an apple, and add, "Ah, you know I'm going to the shelter today. Mackie and I are walking in together."

Mom looks up. "Is this getting serious?" she asks. She sounds kind of thrilled.

"Don't know," I say. "I like spending time with her."

Clutching my apple, I flee from the kitchen. Talking about relationship stuff with Mom just seems too dangerous. I don't even know what Mackie and I have going on. And anything I say to my mom could get back to Mackie's mom. Well, that will happen anyway. I run upstairs, find my cell phone, and text Mackie:

do u want 2 go 2 Cisco's? wes is driving 2 the 7:10 ferry jon & erica R 4 sure. mayB angela & wendy

Her reply comes within a few minutes:

Yes! See U in 30. I'll reply 2 Wes.

I return to my notebook, trying to recall everything I know about Greek mythology. We studied Greek and Roman myths in sixth-grade social studies, and I read more from Edith Hamilton's *Timeless Tales of Gods and Heroes* in my sophomore world history class.

I know that myths are man-made stories created to help people understand their lives and what happens around them. Mythical gods gave order and reason to earthquakes, volcanoes, sickness, war, life, and death. Of course, it hasn't escaped me that the gods were mostly sculpted in the image of humans, even if they did throw an occasional lightning bolt or have a horse's body. Creating gods that looked human made it easier for man to feel close to the controllers of his destiny.

I can understand why Mackie might think my interest in Akeso is a long shot. But almost every religious mythology also establishes a direct link between animals and gods. Among the twelve major Greek gods, most were connected with specific animals. As the supreme god, Zeus' sacred animals were the eagle and the bull. Athena, the goddess of reason and war strategy, claimed the snowy owl. Poseidon, who rules the seas, was connected with horses and dolphins. Aphrodite, goddess of love, was represented by a dove, and Artemis, goddess of the hunt, often appeared with a deer. What if Mackie's ancestors actually had some special healing abilities with animals, and she'd inherited their genetic code?

At one thirty, I jog up our driveway to wait for Mackie. She waves from a distance, and I feel a now familiar rush of happiness inside me.

"Hi," Mackie says, and gives me a quick hug. I hold out my hand. She takes it as we walk along the quiet road.

"So, any news?" I ask.

"My parents have no records of our family coming from the Mediterranean region. Sorry."

"I'm just looking for whatever might explain what's going on. I guess it was pretty out there," I reply, trying hard to keep impatience out of my voice.

Mackie squeezes my hand. "I understand if you think all of this is too weird. If someone told me that they could heal animals just by showing up, I'd think they were either making it up or weird."

"I know you're not lying about the animals, because I've seen them at the shelter when you're around. I was there with you and the orca. It's not weird. It's wonderful. I wish I could do what you do."

"Okay, but what if there isn't an explanation? Maybe I've just grown into this and we're not going to understand it."

I consider that one for a few seconds. "Could be. Maybe it's part of evolution. The strong survive. Maybe that's you and the animals. You've evolved to help them," I say, trying to fit the puzzle pieces together.

Mackie lowers her eyes and shakes her head.

I don't want to let go of her hand. If only we had more time to walk together.

When we arrive at the shelter, we sit on top of an old wooden picnic table located on the side lawn. A chill in the air draws us together, though we don't say much. I want to be with her for a long time.

"Who's playing tonight?" Mackie asks.

"Some group Wes thinks we should hear. I feel like getting off the island, you know what I mean?"

"Yeah. Seattle can be fun."

"Brody hasn't given you any crap since the dance, has he?" I ask.

"No. Maybe he got the message."

"Yeah, well, Brody can be stubborn. I've seen him get territorial over stuff that no one else cares about. Especially if he thinks someone's messing with him," I say.

"I think this is about him not winning. Like he thinks I'm some kind of prize. Somehow I've made him really upset." Mackie sounds far more understanding than I feel.

"Tough. He can't have something just because he wants it."

"I wonder if Jilly knows what she's getting into."

"She will soon enough," I say and stand up. I don't want to waste any more time on Brody, and we need to suit up.

Entering the shelter through the front door, I look for Beth Williams. Beth graduated from Soltrice High seven years before us and is in grad school at the University of Washington, majoring in biology. She wants to go into research. Beth's tall and very thin with long blonde hair. I've known her for the last two years of Saturdays since she and I were assigned the two to six o'clock shift. Our third always rotates in and out, and sometimes I need a substitute if my sports schedule conflicts.

Is it by chance that Mackie has been scheduled, or has Olivia picked up on Mackie and me liking each other? Or did Mackie ask to work with me? Maybe that's how we came to be working together. I'm about to question Mackie as we walk away from the lockers after putting on our coveralls.

"Hi," Beth says suddenly, looking up at us from the corner of the office where coffee and beverages are kept. "We have a new eagle, Number 27."

"Yeah, Mackie was here when he came in. She went with Gabe to get him," I say.

"Let's have a look," Beth urges. "He's in the Small Flight Cage."

We put on our hats and gloves and follow Beth to the back door. Moving as quietly as possible, we approach the cage. Number 27 is huddled, asleep, on a blanket shaped into a nest near the feed station. Even camouflaged in the folds of the fabric, I can tell he isn't big enough to be fully grown. His talons and head have been wrapped in soft cloth. Since the cloth hasn't been ripped off, and our presence isn't alarming him, I assume he is sedated. The bandages and drugs will likely continue for several days.

In the Large Flight Cage, Number 26 has heard us and unfurls her wings on one of the upper perches. Her head held high, she looks awesome, like a queen ready to halt her subjects should they dare cross her path uninvited. When she locks her eyes on Mackie, all her queenliness relaxes. She pulls her wings in and looks down. I almost expect a curtsy to follow. Mackie, meanwhile, directs her gaze at Number 27, concentrating on him.

Beth motions for us to return to the office, but I know Mackie wants more time outside.

She turns to Beth and asks in a whisper, "Could I have a few more minutes? Just to observe him while he's sleeping? I won't be long."

Beth nods. She and I move inside to attend to the other animals, leaving Mackie with the eagles.

Mackie rejoins us in ten minutes, and acts like nothing has happened. I want to be with her, alone. *What, if anything, has gone down between Mackie and Number 27 today?*

The three of us meet up in the main office, and Beth offers to feed the baby chipmunks. Each of five orphaned infants must be hand fed with a small baby bottle.

Beth leaves, and Mackie and I move toward the supply room, picking up tools to clean the birdcages. With the peahen, a goose, and three crows still in recovery, we have plenty to do. And there's also Diana's cage.

"What happened? Anything?" I ask.

"I tried something new. Since he couldn't look at me, I tried to send him my energy. With most animals I feel like they're pulling something out of me. This time I gave."

"Did it work?"

"After a few minutes he lifted his head and tried to keep it up. So, yeah, I think it did work. At least he knows I'm here."

"What about Number 26, did she do anything?"

"No. Not while I was with Number 27. But after I finished with him, I stayed a few minutes with her. She's really strong now."

"Great! I hope I'm around when Number 27 gets a good look at you," I say.

"He's in bad shape. And he's been given a lot of tranquilizers."

"That's for his own protection. He could wake up, go crazy in the cage, and hurt himself."

"I know. I just wish he weren't so out of it."

We resume our chores. All of the birds love having Mackie around and chirp brightly when we move them to clean their cages.

Mackie is her usual calm self, but once I find her looking closely at the peahen. They have a conversation with their faces, and the peahen coos.

When we're back in the hallway, I ask, "What was that about? Between you and the hen?"

"She's used to being around humans, but no one like me. She's curious."

A peahen is curious about Mackie? Me, too!

When our shift ends, we say goodbye to Beth and leave from the front door. Mackie and I need to be ready in forty minutes when Wes picks us up. We jog to the T in the road, and she splits off to her house. I run home for the last two minutes.

In our house, I detect the unmistakable aroma of pizza and cruise into the kitchen.

"Mom, how much time before we eat?"

"The pizza should be done in twenty minutes."

I have time for a shower, and can eat pizza in the car if I cut the time too short.

I take a shower, throw on clean jeans and a dark red T-shirt that Mom says make my eyes look more green than gray, and pull out a blue sweat jacket. Then I put my school ID, driver's permit, and some money in my pocket. I am club-ready.

After speeding downstairs, I check the hallway clock. There are only about five minutes left before Wes is due to arrive. Entering the kitchen at a trot, I stop at the oven and squint inside. The pizza looks ready.

"Mom!"

"I'm right here," she says, stepping back into the kitchen from the pantry. "Go ahead. You can slice the pizza. I'll get Dad and Justin."

I manage to eat one large piece and take another out with me to the front porch in a napkin. Yeow! Hot pepperoni has fried the inside of my mouth. As I lick my lips and wish for something cold to drink, Wes slams his BMW to a stop in front of our house. Angela and Jon are already in the car. We still have to pick Mackie up before meeting everyone else on the boat.

Everything goes according to plan. Wes even finds a parking space close to the boat. On the ferry, we join up with Ty and Wendy. Ty turns to Wes. "Okay, who's playing tonight?" he asks.

"Do you remember that montage group we heard last year? They fused a slammin' bass with dark keyboards and had that short chick singer? They joined up with Cloud Bank six months ago. That's who we're going to hear!" Wes says.

"Oh yeah!" Ty and Jon chorus.

Once in Seattle, we take a bus to Cisco's, getting off within a block of the club. We are late arriving for a hot-ticket group. The doors opened about a half hour earlier, but luckily there is still seating inside for us.

Cisco's has lots of tables and chairs, though once the band starts playing everyone will be on their feet. A dance floor is located right under the stage. Since Cisco's is an all-ages club, when a good band plays the place can get packed. But even with lots of people bumping into each other, Cisco's is like most everything Northwest: friendly-cool and laid back.

We sit at a round table on the side, about two-thirds of the way back from the stage and against the wall. Bounding with excitement, Wes takes off to say hello to some guys he knows at another table, Angela in tow.

A waitress shows up to take our order.

"What would you like?" she asks.

"We'll have two pitchers of root beer and three baskets," Wendy answers.

I like her take-charge attitude. The root beer will be a cold relief for my pizza-scorched mouth, and the baskets will come loaded with thick-cut, herbed sweet potato fries. That's another thing all of us like about Cisco's: cold drinks and carbohydrate sticks.

I give Wendy a smile and mouth the words "thank you."

Mackie nudges me. "Do you know anyone else here?"

"I don't think so."

Cisco's is a place for Seattleites to hang. The hall was a nightclub originally, so it still has a bar with a long wall mirror and bar stools. But the alcohol is gone and the sound system has been upgraded.

Mackie and I talk with Ty and Wendy until the food arrives, then everyone munches as the band finishes its sound check. I make sure the fries have cooled before putting even one in my mouth.

When the music starts, it is hot. The bass is so heavy that I feel sound waves ripple through my body. I see Mackie open her eyes wide, surprised at the strong vibration. People around us jump up and dance, some crazier than others. We stand, swaying to the beat, and watch.

At the end of the first half hour, the band takes a few minutes to change up some of their instruments. Mackie and I look at each other and grin. As Wes offers his opinions about the music, I slide my chair closer to Mackie.

"Do you like them?" I ask.

"The lead singer sounds fantastic. How can she hit those high notes, and then get so low right away?" she says, her eyes sparkling. "And the energy is . . . Wes was right."

"Yeah," I say, putting my arm around the back of her chair. "It's cool. Wish we had something like this on the island." Mackie nods her agreement.

When the band resumes, their pace is still white-hot. Soon everyone in the club stands up, stomping to the beat. I put an arm around Mackie's waist and she does the same with me. Hot? More like flash point.

At the end of the first hour, our waitress shows up again, and we order another pitcher of root beer and ask for water. Mackie turns to talk with Erica, and I make my way to the restroom. Heading back to our table, I see him. Brody.

He stands talking with some guys I don't know. He has on his Soltrice High letter jacket and pokes a finger in one guy's chest. His face is red. I scan for Jilly, but can't find her. That isn't good. What is he doing here? His being at the club doesn't compute for me. Cisco's is pretty tame for Brody.

I walk back to the table, and feel edgy with worry. Mackie is gone.

Erica sees me and waves. "Mackie and Wendy are in the ladies' room."

"Oh, thanks." I feel relief pour through my body. *Has Brody seen her? Probably.* We have a big table that would draw his attention.

I half listen as Wes describes another band scheduled for Cisco's next month, but keep my eyes glued to the opening of the ladies' room. When Mackie and Wendy walk out, I look over at Brody. He is clearly watching for someone. He smirks when he sees Mackie, and turns back to his friends. My muscles tense like springs.

Mackie stops to talk with Erica before sitting down next to me. I still feel jittery about the look I saw Brody give Mackie. *Does she know why he's here?*

"Ah, your former friend is here tonight," I say, trying to stay cool.

With a cute smile, she leans forward and rests her hand on my knee. "Who? Where?" she asks.

I don't answer her because the MC begins announcing Cisco's calendar of upcoming bands.

"It doesn't matter," I say, and take her hand in mine.

Brody has moved away from the juice bar and I can't see where he's gone. Maybe it doesn't matter. *Is Brody here by coincidence?* He doesn't associate with any of my friends, so how could he know that we would be here tonight?

"When we get back to the island, do you want to come to my house? We could watch a late movie or something," Mackie suggests.

"Sounds good," I say, looking straight into her happy eyes. I am so, so lucky.

Then the band starts to play again and I loose track of any worries about Brody as Mackie stands and sways in time to the beat with me. The music replaces all of my worries with waves of surging guitar and keyboard.

At the end of the first set, we leave the club and head eight blocks over and downhill to the ferry. By skipping and speed walking, we arrive at the dock just in time to make the boat. Everyone is in great form. The music has jacked us up. *Our energy can take over the world!*

Wes drops Ty off first, and then drives us to Mackie's house.

"Be good," Wes warns me. "You, too, missy," he adds, pointing both of his index fingers at Mackie.

She blows him an air kiss, laughs and says, "I'm not making any promises, but thank you so much for driving."

Mr. Spence walks out of the kitchen and calls to us, "How about it? Want to watch a classic film? We're just about to see another of the Pink Panther movies. One with Peter Sellers."

"Oh, those are the best," says Mackie, clapping her hands.

We both nod. I've seen two other Pink Panther movies, and they were hilarious.

I pull out my cell phone, call my mom, and speak in a rush. "Hi. Mackie and I are back at her house. I'm going to stay and watch a film. I'll be late, okay?"

"Ask your folks if they'd like to join us," Mr. Spence calls out. "Plenty of popcorn for every one."

"Mr. Spence wonders if you and Dad want to come over, too," I say, biting my lip.

"No, honey. I'm tired and Dad's already asleep. Be quiet when you come in," Mom says.

"Sure."

"Did you have fun at the club?" she asks.

"Yeah, it was great. I'll be quiet. 'Bye," I say, as we move to sit at the end of the great room with a big screen.

Mrs. Spence says hello to me as Noelle races to take her favorite chair. Mackie and I sit together on a small couch, and her parents sit near us on another.

This is the first time I've been with her family in one room since Mackie and I started seeing each other. It feels weird, but not too bad at the same time. Since I've known the Spences for years, I'm sort of okay. *Her parents aren't acting any differently.* I want to put my arm around Mackie. Will they accept my new role in her life?

Mackie solves the problem. She nudges me with her shoulder, then reaches over to hold my hand. Just like that, we announce that we're more than friends. No one acts differently toward us, and I relax as the movie begins. In a few minutes, I put my arm around her shoulder. Soon, all of us are laughing at Inspector Clouseau and his sidekick, Cato.

The movie finishes around one o'clock. But I'm still keyed up from the day. Mackie's parents say goodnight and Noelle drags herself off, making a ferret face at us as she leaves.

Mackie and I walk outside to the front porch. The night has turned cool and I shrug into my jacket, then pull Mackie in and wrap it around her, too.

She stretches up and whispers in my ear, "It was fun tonight, but I always feel good with you. It doesn't matter what we do."

As we kiss, I believe she is right. Being around Mackie is *the best.* I run home knowing I've never been happier. *I love her.* There it is. The feeling I have for her is love. In fact, it feels great that she means everything to me.

CHAPTER 8

Sunday morning I jolt awake from another dream about Mackie and dark water, but this time she calls out to me for help. It's really more of a nightmare than a dream.

I shake my head and try to get rid of the image of Mackie and the darkness, but the pleading look she had on her face in the nightmare stays with me. Reaching for my cell phone, I send her a message:

gr8 nite HRU?

I'm trying to make it a friendly question. She doesn't answer right away, so I get dressed and head downstairs to see about breakfast.

But first I see Mom, alone, in the family room working with a sketchpad. She has three studios to teach this semester and spends Sunday mornings on her own work.

"Hi," I say.

She looks up, startled.

Jeremy. What movie did you see?"

"It was a Pink Panther film. There's this scene where Inspector Clouseau and Cato demolish a hotel room that's amazing. Were all Peter Sellers' movies from the '60s and '70s that funny?"

"You know, that was before my movie time, too. But maybe we should see some of those. You've talked about the Pink Panther films before."

"Yeah, I think you and Dad would like them. Justin, too."

"Okay. How are you and Mackie getting along?"

I squirm. "Fine. We're fine. When's brunch?" I ask.

"In about an hour. Do you need something now?"

My stomach growls. "Yeah, maybe a little."

"Then have some fruit and yogurt."

The rest of the day, I am out of it, as in dragging-myself-around out of it. With two late nights in a row, I've hit my sleep wall. After brunch, I take a nap, and wake to find a message from Mackie that she'll meet me at the shelter. We have no new intakes, which is good, because both Mackie and I look like two-toed sloths, moving in slow motion through our chores. After our shift ends, we push ourselves out the main door and walk home slowly. After dinner, I finally get to my homework, and am in bed by nine o'clock on a Sunday night.

The week flies by. Monday, seated next to Mackie at lunch, I think about my now serene world. I had to look that word up for one of our literature assignments. Serene: peaceful, calm, untroubled. That's how I feel sitting next to her. Okay, when I first see her, my heart thunders like it's next to my ears, but I've become used to that.

Wednesday night, Mackie and I study French together at her house. Noelle looks bored, so we must be doing something right.

Friday after school, Soltrice High hosts a triangular meet with Seattle Prep and O'Dea. Before the meet, at lunch, Mackie invites me to have dinner with her. She has to stay home with Noelle because her parents are taking a late afternoon ferry to have dinner in Seattle and attend some play with friends.

At the meet, my time isn't as fast as at Riley City Park, but it's decent. Brody has continued to ignore me during the week's practices, and our truce holds during the race.

When I walk into the Spences' house, Noelle announces with swirling hand flourishes, "Jeremy, you're in for an extreme dining experience because I have taken the time to customize our pizza."

I throw Mackie a puzzled look. "Customize?"

"Don't get her started, please!" Mackie says, but it's too late.

Noelle begins, in full, Suffering Southern Belle performance style, to describe an addition made to the extra-large frozen pizza.

"Firstly, my dear sister and I disagree on how a pizza pie should taste. But then, my sister has tastes that are quite ordinary."

Mackie raises her eyebrows, folds her arms across her chest, and cocks her head at Noelle. In animal language, this would mean, "Caution. I don't like what I'm hearing."

Noelle continues. "And so, sir, I have taken it upon myself to make this a far more rarified and tasty offering. I've added chewy pieces of succulent baby toes. This is going to be one fabulous pizza. It's going to be the best ever," she says, clapping her hands together and looking at me with glee.

Turning to Mackie, I ask, "So what kind of pizza are we having?"

"Pepperoni with extra cheese," she responds, shaking Noelle by both arms and laughing. "My 'dear sister' hasn't touched this pie."

I sigh in relief. The idea of damaging a perfectly good pizza sends shivers through me.

Noelle tosses her head, turns dramatically, and sits down. "Well I never!" She likes to have the last word.

While the pizza bakes, Mackie pulls us away from Noelle for a private conversation.

"How did it go today?" she asks.

"Good. We took the meet. Coach seemed happy."

"That's very good. What about Brody? Is he still being a jerk?"

"We don't talk. Is he still bothering you?"

"Not as much as usual. Maybe he's moved on with Jilly. It's been a relief to not have him lurking around. But he still sends me messages. You know, he acts like he's a great guy, but he can be really rude." Mackie wrinkles her nose.

I'm not sure what she's referring to, but asking would mean more time spent on Brody. It's enough for me to know that she is finished with him. Still, what has he been writing to her that is 'rude?'

Mackie's phone music jingles, interrupting us.

"Hi, Jen. What's up, cookie? Hey, Jeremy's with me. Okay if I put us on speaker?"

Mackie taps her phone so I, too, can hear Jennifer's excited voice. "Kyle Davenport's having a par-taaaay!" Jen sings. "And he said it was okay for me to invite everyone."

"What's the occasion?" I ask. On the island there are parties and there are *parties*.

"One of his parents' jumpers won a big title this week. They're having a celebration tonight, and Kyle and his brother are asking their friends, too."

"This isn't a dinner, is it?" Mom says I have a way of looking a gift horse in the mouth, meaning that instead of saying "thank you" I ask more about the offer or gift. I am really on it tonight. I glance at Mackie. She doesn't seem offended.

"Not dinner. We'll hang out in the practice barn. Kyle's uncles play in a band and Wes says they're really good. He'll be there."

I keep looking at Mackie, who seems much calmer than Jen about going to this party.

"What do you think?" Mackie mouths.

"How about we get back with you in a few minutes?" I ask Jen.

"Okay, but you guys have to come. It's going to be lots of fun," she says.

After Mackie hangs up, Noelle gives us a big smile. "You two go ahead. I can take care of myself."

"I don't think so. You know we'll both be in trouble if I leave you alone," Mackie says. "But the party sounds like fun and the Davenports have amazing horses. I'll call Mom." Mackie taps her phone. Her face brightens. *Mrs. Spence must still be having dinner.*

"Mom. Everything's okay. Jen called. One of the Davenports' horses won a blue ribbon this week, and Kyle's family is celebrating. Yeah, it's wonderful. Jeremy and I are invited, too." She is quiet for a bit. "Yes, I know. Jeremy's with me, and I think Wes can pick us up. Jen sounds like she's inviting everyone. I'll be back by eleven. Okay?"

Another pause.

"Noelle. Mom wants to talk with you," Mackie says, looking happy and handing her phone to her sister.

"Hi Mom," Noelle says, in what I've come to recognize is her 'I'm a responsible, young-adult-now' voice. "I could call Mia and see what she's doing. Uh-huh, right, I know. Right away."

While Noelle phones her friend, I call my mom. "Mom. Mackie and I are invited to the Davenports' house tonight. One of their horses won some prize. Is it okay to go?"

"You're sure that there will be adults there? Kyle's parents know about this right?" Mom replies.

"Yeah, it's their party, and there will be lots of adults, like Kyle's uncles and other people."

"Who's driving? You need to be home by eleven."

"I'll see if Wes can pick us up. Mackie has to be home by eleven, too, so I don't think that will be a problem."

"All right. Be safe."

Meanwhile, Noelle is back on the phone with her mother. Mission accomplished. We will all go out this evening, Mackie and I to Kyle's, and Noelle to Mia's house.

"Do you want me to find Wes?" Mackie asks.

"No, I'm on it," I reply, grinning. "Good thing Wes likes to drive." I type:

am at mackie's can we catch a ride 2 kyle's

Wes' reply is immediate:

CU @ 8.

Mackie and Noelle have moved into the kitchen to cut the pizza, which smells fantastic, into pieces. With relief, I see that it looks like a normal pie. No customizing. I've just finished wolfing down a third slice when we hear Wes' trademark downshift and sliding stop.

"The last time Wes was here, my dad asked him if he was being scouted by NASCAR," Mackie says, as we start out of the kitchen. I grin and nod.

"Yeah, my dad said something about that, too." I'd like to have a car and slide to a stop like Wes.

Mackie looks at Noelle. "When Mia's mom picks you up, don't forget to lock the front door," she says.

Noelle rolls her eyes. "Okay, Mom."

Mackie pulls a dark blue jacket off a clothes tree in the foyer, and we head out into the night air, ready for action.

"Jeremy! Mackie!" Wes sings. "We're picking Angela up. Ty just got home, so he'll be late. Maybe Wendy's coming, too. I don't know. Jen called everyone. This should be big. Have you guys been to the Double D?"

"I have," Mackie says. "We go to their harvest dinners at the end of October. The horses are beautiful, but I like the lambs. They're really cuddly. Noelle tried to put one in our car once and my mom was ready to kill her. Noelle, not the lamb."

"Our end-of-season soccer team parties have been there. It's a cool place." I add.

When we pull up to her house, Angela waits on her front porch. Her dad comes out of the house and walks with her to our car, looks us over, and speaks to Wes. "There won't be any drinking or drugging at this party, right?"

"No, sir. It's Kyle's parents' party. So there'll be lots of adults around," Wes says.

"Okay, eleven o'clock young lady," Angela's dad stands in the drive, watching us leave with his hands on his hips.

"My dad," Angela murmurs.

Sitting in front with Wes, I turn to him while the girls talk.

"Does Spooner's party still have your parents upset? My mom asks me all the time now about drugs and drinking," I say.

"Yeah. Well, there's a lot of stuff out there. But, I mean, it would be stupid, anyway. Hey, did you hear that Shawn was pulled over this week?"

"What for?"

"He was driving home after football practice; a cop tailed him halfway to his house. He wasn't doing anything wrong. The cop stopped him and he had to show his license. But he didn't get a ticket."

"So, he's just driving, and he gets pulled over?"

"He didn't get busted because there was nothing. I mean, it's Shawn. The guy's so clean he's like soap," Wes says.

The island police don't trust high school students. This is partially understandable, because the cops know kids have easy access to drugs. But over the years they've indiscriminately leaned on everyone, hassling students just off school grounds, stopping them for nothing when they're driving, and busting up perfectly legit gatherings after school on the pretense that they're "too loud."

Angela interrupts us. "I have a question. Will this mainly be the soccer team?"

"There'll be lots of guys from the team, but Kyle would invite everyone," Wes says.

I nod at Wes. That's Kyle. He proposed our school start a Student Mediation Board. Students in trouble for minor offenses sit with the student board to figure out how to make things right. Kyle has been like our own United Nations. He can talk with anyone.

Pulling into the Davenports' long driveway, we pass under the tall Double D metal arch, and park with other cars on a sun-dried, grassy field near one of the barns. As we head for the house, I check things out. I've always liked the ranch. The main house is a two-story, red brick building with a wraparound porch. There are three barns: one for the horses, a second for indoor riding, and a third for the cows, sheep, chickens, and goats. Out of sight, an acre-sized manmade pond sits at the low end of the property.

When we get closer to the porch, I see lots of people I know, including some parents. Kyle is talking with two members of our soccer team, so I lead our group over to say hello.

"Hi, Jer," Kyle calls out as soon as he sees us.

"Hi, hey this looks great," I say.

"Kyle, do you know Angela?" Wes asks. Kyle shakes his head. "Kyle, Angela; Angela, Kyle. I hear your uncles might play tonight. Any chance of that happening?"

"There's no way to stop my Uncle Drew. When there's a crowd, he's going to play. And when Uncle Drew plays, so does Uncle Bob. So I hope you're down with gypsy jazz."

Forget the championship horses. Wes raises his fists over his head and flaps them like *he's* just won the first-place ribbon. Live music is his idea of celebrating.

I put my hand on Mackie's arm, and she giggles. There is a good vibe everywhere. Fiddle music flows from outdoor speakers. I point toward a big tub of soft drinks near a table covered with appetizers. We walk over and pull out cold cans of citrus sparkling water. Then we slip into the crowd.

The air feels mild and I see fleecy cirrus clouds in the south sky with a smattering of stars. Since it's cloudy, it shouldn't get too cold. *Perfect.* Mac and I put an arm around each other's waists and are soon joined by Ty and Wendy.

Jen bounces over, giving us a cheeky smile.

"Hey! Anyone want to go to the barn and see the cute little billy goats?" she asks.

"What? I didn't see any freshmen around," Ty observes while turning his neck as if trying to locate one.

"Be nice," Jen warns him, then floats away to greet someone further in the crowd.

Adults sit on chairs on the house porch, sipping from wine glasses and beer mugs. It looks like some of the Davenports' employees are serving. I see one or two people our age eying the drinks set-up on the porch, but no one approaches the tables.

At around nine o'clock, Mr. Davenport swings a bar inside a hanging, metal triangle to get everyone's attention. "Leigh and I are so pleased that all of you could come out tonight to help us celebrate Chester T. Ford's win at Lexington." He pauses for appreciative applause for Chester T.'s win, grins, and continues. "Help yourselves to food and beverages. My brothers Drew and Bob are favoring us this evening with their special brand of musical entertainment. So let's head over to the practice barn and get them started."

I stroll with Mackie toward the middle barn. Inside, bales of hay have been scattered for seating around an oval riding ring. A stand of bleachers is at the far end. Along the ring railing, Drew and Bob tune their guitars. I've heard Kyle's uncles play before, at the island's summer parks concert series. They're members of a larger gypsy jazz band named the Snape Shakers. The complete band is made up of a lead guitar, a violin, two rhythm guitars, and a bass.

Suddenly, a man carrying an old upright bass walks through the barn doors. Drew and Bob look at each other in amazement. Their bass player seems to have shown up unexpectedly.

It takes about ten minutes for people to enter and quiet down. Jon and Erica sit on a bale of hay next to Mackie and me. Jen walks in with, to my surprise, Ryan. I've never been around him socially before, only with the cross-country team. *This is new.*

Mackie gives me with an amused smile and whispers, "Uh oh. Does Ryan know Jen very well? Does he know what he's in for?"

I shake my head. Ryan is kind of a loner and Jen is, well, she can be really out there. But he doesn't look nervous, and Jen has quieted down, reining in her big personality

The musicians test their mics. "Hello, I'm Drew and this is my brother, Bob. I'm pleased to say that with us tonight is a third member of the Snape Shakers Gypsy Jazz Band, the man who keeps our beat rocking, Otto Millard. Otto's going to cook things up for us on string bass. And that's what we're here to do. Get you all warmed up with some hot gypsy jazz. The hotter the better, right, Bob? Otto? Okay, boys. One! Two! Three! Hit it!"

During the first song, Mr. Davenport and his wife move to the center of the riding ring and begin dancing. Others soon join them. By the band's third number, almost everyone dances or stands swaying to the music.

Mackie smiles at me slyly, pulls me by my hand off our hay bale, and says, "I know you can dance!"

As we make our way to the edge of the dancers, I see Jon and Erica already on the floor. Jen has pulled Ryan out to dance, too. I find myself using some of the same steps I learned at Sadie One. It feels just right to hold, push, and spin to the music.

Mackie looks really sweet. Her hair flares out when she twirls, and her eyes glow with excitement. She wears a shirt that shows the curves in her hips. The colors in her rings throw off sparkles in the light as we twirl around the dance circle. We both have on blue jeans and boots, which turns out to be a smart move because people stomp down hard on the sawdust-covered floor.

Kyle's uncles and Otto play for about forty-five minutes before announcing a last song before they take a break. Mackie and I stay on the floor the whole time. The last dance is slow. Fast is fine, but slow dancing with Mackie has to be my favorite. She leans into me and rests her head on my chest. I hold her hand and tuck my elbow. As Mrs. Walton at the shelter likes to say, we are "just lovely."

During the band's break, we walk outside to the sound of recorded fiddle music. Most of our last year's soccer team has arrived, including Brody. He's with Cole and a couple of other seniors. Jilly isn't with him. *Where is she?* Mackie leaves to find some water for us to drink. Recalling what happened at Sadie One, I keep a lookout for her return. Just when I start to get worried, she strolls up, hands me a bottle of water, and links her arm through mine.

That's when I see Jilly. She's about twenty feet away from Brody with her eyes on Mackie. More accurately, with her shooting-daggers-eyes on Mackie. Glancing at Brody, our eyes meet and he sneers. Mackie and I have an audience. *A hostile audience.*

Wes, Angela, Jon, and Erica join us, laughing about something.

Wes says, "Drew and Bob told us about the Snape Shakers' southern California tour. In January, they'll be playing in sun and seventy degrees. Man, I want to be there."

Kyle joins us and asks, "What do you think?"

"Get your uncles back in the barn because I could listen to them all night!" Wes crows.

Knowing Wes' affinity for music, he isn't exaggerating.

Then, with no warning, the Soltrice Island police show up. A blue and white car with overhead flashing lights works through the crowd outside the first barn.

Everyone stops talking. Fast. Mr. Davenport steps down from the house porch to meet them.

"Officers, what can I help you with?" Kyle's dad asks, his voice strained but polite as the police exit their car.

"I'm Officer Schmidt. This is Officer Clary," says the tall policeman with his hand on the butt of his holstered gun. "We got a call from one of your neighbors about noise. They'd like you to turn it down."

"Okay. I'll ask the boys to lower their volume. Anything else?"

"Nope."

Officer Schmidt squints at the tables on the house balcony.

"I see you're serving. Of course, no one under 21 years of age has had a drop. Right?"

"There's been no underage drinking tonight," Mr. Davenport says. His polite smile is gone.

"Sure. I'd be mighty careful if I was driving home tonight," Officer Schmidt says loudly. He screws his mouth into a twisted smile as he scans those of us standing near the porch.

Mr. Davenport now has a frown on his face.

After the police climb back in their car, Jon turns to me.

"Once again, Soltrice Island's finest investigate criminal activity. What do you guys want to do?" he asks.

"Let's go back and listen to more music," Wes says. Angela nods. So that's what we do. But the buzz is all about the police showing up at the party. After playing for another hour, the band puts their instruments away. Wes picks me out of the crowd and waves me to him.

"Time to go. Where's Mackie?" he asks.

"She was just here," I say. I look around, but can't find her. "I'll look for her. You know every cop on the island will be on the roads waiting for us when we drive out of here," I say.

"Right, a perfect night for a little head cracking," Wes says.

He's over stating things, but the police have a reputation of bullying high school students. And adults aren't out of their reach, either. We had seen that tonight.

I finally see Mackie and Angela and wave to them. The girls have been talking with Jennifer and Ryan. Mackie nods to me and they join us. We leave the warm glow of the barn for the cool night air and Wes' car.

Mackie doesn't say much on the ride back to her house. When we arrive, we say our goodnights to Wes and Angela. Mackie looks worried as we stand on the front porch.

Placing my hand on her shoulder, I ask, "What's wrong?"

"I can't find my phone. It's not like it can't be replaced, but I have everyone's numbers and some saved messages on it. Photos, too."

"Where do you think you lost it?"

"It must have been in the barn. I turned it off when we sat down and didn't use it after that."

"Maybe someone found it and will call you. Or maybe they gave it to Kyle's parents."

"Yeah, this is really bugging me." Mackie looks tired.

"Let me try Kyle," I offer, sending him a message asking whether Mackie's cell phone has been found. The answer comes back fast:

No cell here.

"Don't worry. Someone will find your phone. You should call Kyle tomorrow to find out if anyone found it. Or maybe his parents already have it," I say.

I tell her the number. Mackie repeats it back. Then she yawns.

"See you tomorrow at the shelter," I say, feeling a sleepy yawn-echo roll inside me.

"No. Olivia shifted my schedule because some new volunteers signed up. Since I already work weekdays, she's not assigning me any more weekend days."

I'm disappointed. Working with Mackie on the weekends has been great for two reasons: I can be with her, and I can observe how the Mackenzie Effect works on animals. How else will I figure out how and why she can do so much for them?

Mackie takes my hand and, with a smile, says, "It's not like I can just tell them that the animals will heal faster if I'm around. Maybe something will happen and Olivia will put me back on weekends with you."

I feel a little better.

I know I have to go, but I want to be clear about something. "I like dancing with you," I say. "Tomorrow, after I finish at the shelter, do you want to do something?"

She nods.

"Okay, I'll call you. Hey remember, they're releasing Number 26 tomorrow."

"I know. I'll be there," she responds with sleepy eyes.

With that, I bend down, kiss her, and run home to make my curfew.

Chapter 9

Saturday morning, I rise from bed early, around seven thirty, and wander down to the kitchen. Justin and Mom sit at the table eating breakfast. Mom will leave soon, to teach her weekend class.

"Jeremy, I heard there was a problem last night," she says.

So my mom heard about the Davenports' busted-up party through her own network.

"Well, not really. The police showed up for a few minutes," I say, trying to unknot my woolly brain.

"Why?"

"I guess one of the Davenports' neighbors thought it was too noisy. Kyle's uncles and this Otto guy had amps plugged in, so maybe the music was loud. I don't know. It seemed okay."

"Were kids drinking alcohol?"

"Mom. Nothing happened other than the police came in and busted up an outstanding party. It doesn't seem fair. It was only music," I say, as I pull out yogurt, milk, and orange juice from the fridge.

"Well, judges don't necessarily go by what's fair. They go by what's legal."

Point to Mom.

"Yeah, I know," I say. "Something can be illegal and not be fair. And what's legal might not be fair, either." Fairness and legality have become hard for me to figure these days.

Mom nods, but it's too early for this conversation. My brain feels frozen in space, or maybe I just need more sleep.

"Jeremy, you know that if there's a citation concerning alcohol or drugs on your high school record, the people who award scholarships won't consider you," Mom says.

She is really upset!

"It's okay. They didn't write my name down," I say, trying to soothe her. "Really, I think the cops are bored. Wes said Shawn Fielding was stopped on the highway after school yesterday, and he wasn't doing anything wrong. He didn't even get a traffic ticket."

"Did people dance?" she asks.

The shift in subject relieves me.

"Yeah. It was fun. People were up. Even Ryan danced. With Jen."

"Well, Jen's a nice girl. I'm glad you had a good time. Did Mackie have fun, too?"

"She said she did. We're supposed to do something tonight, but I'm not sure what."

I can't tell if Mom can hear me over the cereal bowls' clattering as she places them in the dishwasher.

Justin, meanwhile, adjusts his earbuds and moves his lips with no words coming out. He's been listening to a book on tape while Mom and I talk. When he stands, it hits me that he's taller. My tadpole of a brother is growing legs.

I trudge upstairs. Propping my feet on my desk, I review my homework assignments. I have about four hours of studying to do over the weekend. After reading for about two hours, I go back downstairs to make lunch using leftovers foraged from the refrigerator and freezer. Dad walks in and asks if the Davenports called their attorney when the police showed up without a warrant. I say I don't know. We leave it at that.

When I arrive at the shelter, someone has attached bright blue balloons to a post at the top of the driveway. Certain areas in the building have signs posted that read 'Restricted, No Admittance' and an outside table has been set up for food and beverages. Best of all, there are five additional volunteers on hand for the afternoon.

It's all about Number 26's release. Her shoulder has mended completely, a Fish & Wildlife officer tagged her for tracking yesterday, and an announcement about the release has gone out to volunteers and the public. The shelter is ready to celebrate setting Number 26 free.

Beth, already in work coveralls, waves to me. "Hi Jeremy," she says. "We'll do some cage cleaning before the release and show our new volunteer, James Monroe, what to do. He's only had four hours of orientation and training."

I wonder if he's related to James Monroe, the fifth president of the United States.

Beth organizes us to first clean the coyote cage, then the inside birdcages. Close to three o'clock, we will join the other volunteers and guests outside to watch Number 26 fly away.

I worry because I haven't heard from Mackie, but she told me days ago, and again last night, that she plans to be at the ceremony.

We work on cleanup and feeding chores until around two forty-five, when people begin showing up for the release. Because Number 26 has been with us for about a year, and because she is a bald eagle, a protected bird, this event is a big deal. Fully recovered, it's likely she will fly back to her nesting territory, near the shelter.

I see Mrs. Walton speaking with Olivia and join them.

"Hi Mrs. Walton. Olivia. Looks like a good day for this," I say.

"Right you are, Jeremy Number 26 certainly deserves it. She's worked hard to get her wings back." Mrs. Walton twinkles at me.

After many months of work, Mrs. Walton has forged a tight bond with Number 26. She straps into the heavy padding that will allow her to carry the eagle outside of the cage. I doubt that Number 26 would ever try to hurt Mrs. Walton, but eagles talons are strong and sharp, and the shelter has a responsibility to keep volunteers safe. So, she has to wear the protective gear.

At last we are ready. It's three o'clock and about fifty people stand in front of the Large Flight Cage in leaf-dappled afternoon light. I can't see Mackie. Is she somewhere in the crowd? Mrs. Walton walks out with Number 26 folded down and cradled in her arms. Thick padding covers Mrs. Walton's arms and chest. Everyone becomes quiet. *This is an important moment.*

"You've been a fine patient, Number 26, now be a proud, soaring eagle," Mrs. Walton says, as she lifts her arms and pushes Number 26 away from her.

At first Number 26 unfolds her wings, but only jumps away from Mrs. Walton and lands on the ground. She looks back at those of us standing near the Large Flight Cage. She doesn't fly.

Mrs. Walton encourages her by slowly raising her own arms up and down at her sides. "Fly, go on now, fly. Fly."

Then, with only three steps for momentum, Number 26 lifts off the ground with her wings flapping and soars into the woods. A cheer goes up. Everywhere I turn, I see people with glistening eyes. My own eyes are wet, too! That's what makes everything so bright and shiny.

After the ceremony, Gabe shakes Mrs. Walton's hand, and everyone talks and eats cookies and cake brought by volunteers. A Fish & Wildlife officer explains that Number 26 will be tracked constantly for about a month. That way, if she has any trouble, someone can retrieve and help her.

I search for Mackie after the ceremony, but can't find her, which seems odd, because Mac was a big part of Number 26's recovery. And Mackie specifically said that she would attend the release. *Where is she?*

I try her phone, but my call goes to voice mail. "Hi, it's me," I say. "Number 26 just took off. Where are you?" I don't get a response and turn my cell off. We aren't supposed to use our phones around the animals. After everyone leaves, Beth, James, and I finish our cleaning and feeding chores. Animals not on sedatives are more alert because of the noise from the celebration. Number 26's release has been a party for them, too, just not as much fun as for us humans.

James and I take care of the raccoons first.

"Have you been around injured raccoons?" I ask James, as I scoop fresh food into a pail and he shoulders a water jug.

"Never. Where I lived we only saw them at night, and they ran away when they'd see people."

"Where did you live?"

"Idaho. We lived on the backside of a foothill. Elk and moose walked through our yard every day."

"Nice."

Four raccoons greet us with open and alert eyes, rare in the afternoon when they usually sleep. So I use an extension pole to open the food trap and shove in plates of eggs, fruit, and nuts while keeping a safe distance. Most of the raccoons are older babies and adolescents that already have sharp claws on their finger-like toes. Getting near an awake and curious raccoon would be a big mistake.

When we finish, Beth meets us in the hallway.

"The outdoor waterfowl cage is a mess. The birds are really nervous today with all the extra activity," she says. "I can use your help."

This is not my favorite chore because goose poo sticks to everything like goo-glue. The cage and pools have to be thoroughly hosed down several times a week.

While Beth and I settle the three mallards, two Canadian geese, and a sea gull in nearby cages, James uses the jet setting on a hose to spray the interior. We refill the three deep round pools used for bathing. Next, we restock the birds' food containers with lettuce, seed, millet, barley, grubs, and crickets, adding some scratch on the side. Then we bring the birds back and quietly close the door.

"Jeremy," Beth says. "Would you take care of the ducklings and goslings while I show James what has to be done for the baby fox we took in last week?"

As I walk to the baby waterfowl room, I puzzle more about Mackie. I message her:

26s release went GR8 where RU

No reply. Maybe she still doesn't have her phone to see my text. But there are other phones at her house that she could use to call me. *Why isn't she telling me what's going on?*

Ducklings and goslings have their own special, warm interior room. I move the fluffy, young birds to cardboard boxes, enjoying their peeps and nudges for attention. Then I clean their wooden boxes and add fresh pine shavings.

Waterfowl are cuddly, friendly little guys. Being held doesn't terrify them, though they initially try to run away when I go to pick them up. That's hard-wired in their survival system. I stroke each duckling and gosling as I return the birds to their boxes.

But the animals are only temporary distractions. Mackie is on my mind.

I send her another message:

where RU can u talk

If someone found Mac's phone, they should respond, if only to learn how to contact the owner. Or maybe they don't intend to return her phone?

When we finish our work early, Beth, James, and I sit and eat leftover cookies.

"What I already miss is backcountry skiing," James says. "I could take off from our house and within a half mile gain 200 feet. Sometimes I'd take snowshoes, but the snow was deep enough by the end of October that I could ski. Do you ski?"

As Beth and James chat, I pay enough attention to stay in the loop, but worry about Mackie. *What is she doing?*

Close to six o'clock, the next shift of volunteers arrives.

I jog up the shelter's driveway to the road, looking at my phone. Nothing. I run home, partly because I feel cold, and partly because not hearing from Mackie makes me anxious. I feel frustrated because there isn't much I can do. *Get a grip. Settle down.* She will call. Of course she will.

After dinner, Mom asks, "Did you and Mackie decide on what you'll do tonight?"

"I haven't been able to reach her. She lost her phone last night at Kyle's. Guess I'll have to wait for her to call me," I say, feeling glum.

"You could call her mom or dad," Mom suggests.

Now I have a back-up plan. Maybe Mackie is eating dinner. I'll give it another half hour.

After brushing my teeth and taking a shower, I sit on my bed and check my cell phone. Still nothing. I try again:

can u talk

She replies:

Am busy 2nite.

What? I felt bad, like she's slapped me. It's kind of a rude message to send when we agreed last night to do something together this evening. If she didn't want to be with me, why didn't she say so yesterday? I feel an achy hurt, like I'm not wanted.

To counter my black cloud of a mood, I lie back on my pillow, plug in my earbuds, and listen to some tunes Wes sent me. I also begin playing a game on my notebook. "Am busy 2nite." *What is that supposed to mean?* She's never sent a message like that before. Why now?

When Mom flings open my bedroom door and walks in unannounced, I'm completely out of it. She has a frown and looks worried. Motioning for me to take my earbuds out, she sits on the edge of my bed.

"I just spoke with Caitlin. She thought Mackie was with you because Mackie didn't come home for dinner. Do you know where she is?"

"No. Like I told you, we never made any definite plans. She texted me about an hour ago that she was busy. Why does Mrs. Spence think she's here?" I ask.

"I don't know, but you should call her back. She's worried. I think you should help find Mackie. Use my phone so she'll answer." Mom looks tense. I send the number she's picked out.

Mackie's mom answers. "Stephanie?"

"No. It's Jeremy. I don't understand, did Mackie say she would be at our house?"

"Oh, Jeremy, thank you for calling, dear. We've been trying to find her."

"You know she lost her phone last night, right?"

"Yes. She was upset about it this morning. She called Kyle and he didn't have it. After Nick and I left for the farmers' market, Mackie sent us a message that she was leaving to pick her phone up. But she didn't say who had it or where she was going.

"Noelle told us that Mackie left on her bicycle around one o'clock. That was the last any of us saw her. She sent me a message that she was going to the shelter, and then to your house. Did you see her at the shelter?" Mrs. Spence asks.

"Ah, no. She never showed up for the eagle release. Did the message she sent you come from her cell phone?"

"Yes."

"I could ask Kyle if he knows anything new. Maybe someone dropped it by the Davenports' after you left for the market," I suggest, knowing it's a long shot.

"Oh, thank you Jeremy. Please let us know right away if you learn anything," Mrs. Spence says, and we say goodbye.

Mom looks serious. "Mackie's been gone for both lunch and dinner without her parents knowing where she is. That's not like her. Do you know anything about this?"

"No. Like I said, she sent me a message that she was busy tonight. Let me try Kyle."

I tap:

did mackie get her phone from u 2day

I receive an immediate response:

Haven't seen her. Sorry.

Well, it had been worth a try. I try Mackie again:

where R U?

No response. My mom and I look at each other. I try again:

do u want 2get 2gether 2nite

No

My mom's phone buzzes. It's Nick Spence. She puts him on speakerphone.

"Stephanie, I'm terribly sorry to bother you. Was Jeremy able to reach Kyle?"

"Kyle sent a message that he hasn't seen Mackie. We've been trying to figure out where she might be," Mom says.

"We've called everyone. Nobody's seen her. I hate to get the police involved, but we're flat out of options," Mr. Spence says.

"I just sent a message asking if she still wanted to get together tonight, and she wrote 'No,'" I say.

"Just now? This just happened?"

"Yes."

"Well, I don't understand. We're worried that she might have had an accident. You know, lots of people don't pay good attention when they drive. Someone could have hit Mackie on her bike. Down home, we'd have scent dogs looking for her, but up here I've got nothing. And she sends you a one-word message. Just 'No.' Oh, that fries me."

"Uh, it doesn't seem like something she'd do on purpose," I say. Mackie's being gone and not answering her mom and dad's calls really isn't like her.

Oh crap, there might be an explanation no one knows about. She might have had another healing situation like with the orca. Maybe she's physically exhausted now. But since she has her phone back, why not just call someone to pick her up? She could call Jen who has her own car. On the other hand, Mackie has been very clear with me about no one besides us knowing what she can do. Still, it doesn't make sense for her to not have explained where she was when she replied to me. Why the secrecy when she knows I will understand and help her?

It worries me that the Spences have decided to contact the police. That is the last thing Mackie would want. It means she'll have lots of nosy people grilling her about where she's been all day. But why not tell her parents, or me for that matter, that she is okay? *Maybe because she's not okay.*

Mom stares at me after ending the call. "Jeremy, Nick and Caitlin are worried sick. Why isn't Mackie calling them, but sending you text messages?"

"I don't know. It doesn't add up for me, either."

It's nearly eight o'clock and dark outside. After Mom leaves, I pick up my phone and check to see if I've missed a new message. Nothing. Where is she? I try again to reason it out, but none of it makes sense. Then I send a group message to our friends:

we need 2 search 4 mackie who's in?

Their responses come, fast.

From Jen: *Yeah! Let's find her. I can drive.*

From Jon: *I'm in.*

From Erica: *Me 2.*

From Wendy: *I'll help.*

From Ty: *Yes!*

From Wes: *I'll drive.*

My final message: *I'll go with wes and ty*

With more coordinating, Wes and Jen arrange to drive to areas where we know Mackie might ride her bike. Now that we have a plan, I feel a little better. Still, it's not good. Nick Spence said he would call the police, so if Mackie is hurt they will find her. So far, they've found nothing. What if she's hurt and she's crawled away from the road? It doesn't explain her phone message to me. *Why didn't she write more than just 'Am busy 2nite'?*

Fifteen minutes later, Wes' tires spray gravel when he slams to a stop in our drive. Ty sits in the front, so I pop the back door and slide in.

"Jeremy." Wes says. "What's going on? Did you and Mackie have a fight?"

"No," I reply, surprised at his question. "We were supposed to get together tonight, but we didn't have any definite plans."

"She's not just blowin' you off?" Ty asks.

"I don't think so. We didn't have a fight or anything. It was all good last night except that she lost her phone at Kyle's." Ty's wondering if Mackie is staying away from me on purpose hasn't occurred to me. But nothing has added up tonight.

"Okay, then something must be wrong." Wes says it so definitely that my defenses against thinking that something bad has happened to Mackie crash. I shudder. *Not Mackie!*

Wes drives us around the eastern and northern island routes. Jennifer, Wendy, Erica, and Jon search the western and southern roads. I don't know exactly what we hope to accomplish, but it feels better than sitting alone, worrying, at home.

On the north side, something flickers near a curve in the road. *Whew!* It's a deer, moving slowly along the narrow gravel shoulder.

At ten thirty we meet at Jen's house. Everyone is really down. I call my mom to see if she has more news from the Spences. Nothing. The outlook for finding Mackie is getting worse with each passing hour.

"There has to be a good reason she's not home. Mackie doesn't do things like this," Jen says.

"Yeah," Ty agrees. "She's usually the one who gets us out of trouble."

"We've looked everywhere that she would bike. And her parents have contacted half the island. We have to hope she calls and actually talks to someone," Jon sums up.

Wes drops me off at home around eleven o'clock. Mom and Dad are in the kitchen. Mom looks nervous, and Dad looks more serious than I've seen him about pretty much anything.

"Your mom and I are going to bed, but if you hear anything about Mackie wake us up. Okay?" he says.

"Right," I respond, wishing I had brought good news with me.

Once upstairs in my bedroom, I put my face in my hands to wipe away the tears on my cheeks. The last time I cried out of fear was when I was seven years old. Den Webster, the class bully, threw me on the ground and told me he was going to cut me up in little pieces and then flush me down the toilet. But this is different. I'm afraid *for* Mackie, not *of* her. It feels worse, in so many ways.

My phone lights up with an incoming call from a number I don't recognize.

"Hello?"

"Hi, Jeremy? This is Jilly Parker. Do you know who I am?"

"Yeah. You're seeing Brody, right?" I say. *Why is she calling me? And so late?*

"Right. I, um, have you seen Brody tonight?" she asks, in a choked-up voice.

"No. Is he missing?"

"I don't know. I can't find him." She pauses. "I took Mackie's phone last night."

I sit down on my bed and turn the volume up on my phone. Her voice is so faint I have trouble making out all of her words.

"Uh-huh," I say, wanting her to keep talking.

She sniffles, but continues. "I used Brody's phone to make a call at Kyle's and saw all of the times he'd messaged Mackie. I wanted to see if she replied, so I took her cell phone."

"How?" I ask her.

"I took it when she wasn't looking. I was going to put it back on the hay bale after I checked her outgoing log, but Brody grabbed it from me. I asked him why he was writing her so much if they were over. We had a bad fight." Jilly begins to cry.

"So what did Brody do with Mackie's phone?"

"I didn't see him give it back to her, so maybe he still has it."

Huh.

This is a whole new possibility. That Brody is involved.

"When was the last time you saw him?" I ask, hoping to calm her down and get more information.

"Um, at Kyle's party. I got mad and told him he was a liar. Now, he's not talking to me. He's not with Mackie, is he?"

Damn, I hope not!

I try to keep cool, as my hand clenches my phone.

"I don't know, Jilly. But it's not your fault that he's a jerk."

"Okay. Just so you know, I don't have anything against Mackie. She seems nice. She didn't send any replies to his messages."

"Jilly. Where do you think Brody is now?"

"I don't know. He said that his parents and Jake would be gone for the weekend, and we'd have the house to ourselves. We were supposed to have a party tonight. I went there today, but no one was home. I've called around and nobody's seen him. I thought he might be with Mackie, and you knew about it. I'm sorry."

She's crying again. I want to hang up and go find Brody, but not for the reasons Jilly could want.

"Jilly, it's late. I'm sorry but I don't know where he is. Call me if you hear something, okay? And don't worry. Brody always makes sure he's okay."

She mumbles something that sounds like "thanks," and we say goodbye. I end the call and stare at my phone.

Brody took Mackie's cell phone from Jilly in the Davenports' barn. *Does he still have it?* I received texts today from her phone. This is a fact. Maybe Mackie didn't send them, though. Maybe it was Brody?

Brody could have called the Spences' house number to tell Mackie that he had her cell phone. Mackie told her mother she was going to get her phone, and left on her bike. Though she didn't like being around Brody, Mackie would meet him to get her phone back. To do that, she must have been with him some time during the day. Brody, the guy who Mackie said was obsessed with her and tried to make her feel like she owed him something. *Not good. Not good at all!*

I stand in a rush, and run down the stairs. In the hallway, I grab a flashlight, my jacket, and reflector.

It is late, so there is no traffic as I start to run the streets leading to the island's northern point, near Locke's Pass, and then west to Port Claridon. The port is where the Camerons' waterfront home is located. I didn't care about anything but finding Mackie and making sure she's safe. If I have to go through Brody to do that, then I will.

Chapter 10

I was at Brody's house last year, after one of our soccer games. Running the three miles fast, I use the beam of my flashlight and the dim overhead moonlight to follow the streets. A couple of times the uneven asphalt on the road shoulder throws me off balance, and I have to jerk upright to avoid falling.

Finally, I find the tall columns of mortared rocks that look like guards at the top of the Camerons' drive. Like most waterfront homes on the island, their house isn't visible from the road. Before me stretches a long driveway that winds back through the property into blackness.

I gasp for breath as I step off the road and onto the drive entrance. Woods on either side of me make it feel like I'm looking down a tunnel. The front of their yard is dense with salal and tiers of hemlock and cedar trees. I can't see much of anything beyond my small flashlight beam as I walk down the drive. Not wanting to tip off Body that I've arrived, I palm my light to keep the beam dim, and point it at my feet. I move cautiously forward.

Ahead are lights, but only outside, at the front porch and outside of the south wing. The house is huge. It has multiple rooflines, elevated decks, and six entrances. A square, two-story guesthouse sits about one hundred feet off the main house. The guesthouse looks completely dark. Ditto for the third building, a three-bay garage.

I stay close to the main house and slip along to the west entrance facing the water. Light filters around the edges of the kitchen's window blinds. Otherwise, the place appears to be empty.

After shuffling in a low crouch to move beyond the house, I peer through a window inside the detached garage. Brody's red convertible is parked inside with one other vehicle, a sedan that looks like it might belong to his parents.

I make my way back to the house, knowing that homes like the Cameron's have security systems. Experience has taught me electronic surveillance is hard to beat. But I need to find out if Brody is inside the house.

Moving into the main yard with its formal garden and waterfront, I stop behind some low shrubs so I can view the full west face of the house. Because the night is dark, I won't be seen but can monitor any change of lighting inside. Pulling out my phone, I tap in a message to Mackie's phone:

i know where u r

This should get a reaction out of Brody. If he has Mackie's phone.

I wait. There are no changes in the house lights. I move to the east side of the house that faces into the woods. No additional lights have been turned on. Nothing has changed in the house since I sent my text.

What if Brody isn't buying my message? Because we run cross-country and play soccer together, he can spot my bluffs. If I really knew where Mackie was, I'd just show up, not send a message.

I jog around the building to sit on a garden bench off the kitchen entrance. Brody's car is here, so logically he is on the property somewhere. I can't get into the house, but nothing suggests that he's actually in the house. *Where else can he be?* The guesthouse? No. It's dark and looks deserted. Same for the garage. That leaves the grounds. Wouldn't he want to be comfortable inside the house? According to Jilly, Brody's parents and brother are gone for the weekend. So Brody has the run of the place, the whole property for that matter.

Brody. He's a creature of habit. I know that from playing with him. He favors certain repeat moves. But above all, he likes to be the leader. He has to be the guy in control. So, in this house, he'd want to be in rooms where he could see everything around him. All of those rooms have a water view.

I shiver from sitting in my own sweat. *Keep moving.* I walk around the house's corner to the west side and gaze up at the windows. Still no change in the kitchen lights. Turning slowly, I search the lawn and garden. *What am I missing?*

Then I see it. A tiny light pops out just beyond the shoreline, in the water, like a low wattage security spot. The light is on the sailboat at the Camerons' dock! *Is Brody on their boat?*

Again cupping my flashlight's beam, I edge through the flower garden to a stepping-stone walkway. The waterfront is about two hundred feet from the house. The tide is in and it looks like I can walk out on the dock and step into the water. *DARK WATER* I shudder at the words Mackie spelled on the Ouija board. *Focus.*

I strain to hear voices, any sound at all.

The tiny light seems to glow from below deck. Brody could be there. But I can't hear or see him. I need to find out. Moving fast down the stepping stones, it takes only seconds to close in on the gleaming white boat.

Walking on the wooden dock will be more of a challenge. The dock will creak with each of my footsteps. There is no way to disguise my arrival. I move cautiously, hugging the two-sided railing. At the end of the dock, I stand parallel along the starboard side.

During the summer of my freshman year, I took sailing classes through the parks department. But this boat is huge compared to the small Sunfishes I sailed. Stepping tentatively on deck, I listen and still hear nothing but a slight shifting of the boat. *Am I wrong? Brody isn't here?*

Ahead, a lighted stairway at the hatch leads to rooms below. This is the light I saw from the yard. I inch to the opening with my flashlight turned off. There is something sticky on the floor, but it's not slowing me. I focus carefully as I step down the stairs.

Whoa! A man's legs, ending in deck shoes, stick out in the aisle from behind a tall cabinet. Someone is within six feet of me! But there is no sound. They look like Brody's legs. What's he doing? I've made plenty of noise. He should be alert and checking me out.

Holding my breath, I tense for him to make his move. Then I see Mackie's phone on a low table to the right of his legs. *Maybe she is here!* The figure behind the cabinet doesn't move. *Brody?*

"Uh, er . . ." I clear my throat and cough.

No movement from The Legs.

Creeping forward, I stay on guard, ready for him to lunge at me. There's an empty gin bottle on the floor between us. *Has he passed out?* Great. If so, I'll have to rouse him to get answers about Mackie. I peer around the cabinet.

Shit!

It *is* Brody! He has three-inch, parallel cuts ending in puncture wounds covering his head, arms, and chest. His T-shirt is ripped all over. His hair is matted with blood from what look like holes capped with coagulated mounds of blood. Dried blood covers his closed eyelids. I stagger closer.

Alive or dead?

"Bro," I whisper. I try again. "Brody, wake up. Come on, wake up, Bro." I nudge his foot with mine. Still nothing.

Oh shit, crap, shit! He's dead?

I need to find out, but don't want to touch him. I walk around the cabin looking for matches. In a drawer I find a long, butane lighter, the kind used to light gas grills. Moving back to Brody's sickening self, I push, click, and light a flame about two inches under his nostrils. The flame flickers. He's breathing! *Yes!*

I slump against a side chair. As much as Brody disgusts me, I don't want to see him dead. But he is crazy hurt, his skin raked and punctured. Blood is smeared everywhere on him. What happened?

The sticky stuff I stepped in must be blood, and it tops the deck and stairs. *Is someone else on the boat with me? The person who did this to Brody?*

I push my panic down. I have to call for help. What about Mackie? Is she hurt, too? I call out, "Mackie! Come on Mac. Mackie, where are you?" My voice bounces off the walls.

Nothing.

Still calling her name, I make myself concentrate on moving through the cabin. There isn't any blood beyond the main room. That's good. Hopefully, it's all Brody's.

The doors to the rooms farthest forward are wide open. I check them out, including the shower and head. Empty. By this time I am shaking, and can hear my teeth chattering, but not from being cold. The whole place is absolutely beyond crazy. *Brody. Blood. Who could have done this to him?* Fear pushes up against my throat.

Climbing the stairs to the main deck, I call, "Mackie, come on, Mackie. Answer me. Mackie. Mackie."

Silence.

I put my hand in my pocket to pull out my phone when I see a piece of light blue fabric with tiny white dots, torn in a long strip, hanging from a rigging. I step closer. Mackie has a shirt like this. I've seen her wear it lots of times.

Frantically, I pace around the deck. *Has she come and gone, or is she still somewhere on the boat?* I want to find her, more than anything. Brody is alive. He can wait.

Standing mid ship, I rub my eyes and stare out at the water in the bay on the port side. Feeling like a balloon that's slowly losing air, I make myself move. I want to get away from the dark water.

As I step off the boat onto the dock, I hear a sound overhead. It's an eagle's cry. That shouldn't happen. Eagles hunt during the day. They have limited night vision. But right now, an eagle is somewhere near me. *Oh crap!*

I step back onto the boat, fold my hands across my chest to look non-threatening, and look up. I barely find the shape of the bird. It circles above, something eagles do when they're marking territory. Or searching below for prey.

Why is this happening? Is this bird hunting me? I grab a padded cushion from a deck chair and hug it to my chest. The bird spirals just off port. Then it hits me like a lightning bolt, why the puncture wounds on Brody looked so familiar. They're the same size and pattern that I've seen on eagles that have been brought to the shelter after they've been attacked. By another eagle! *Is this bird circling to attack me?*

Moving along the railing, I peer into the calm, dark water. *It's too dark. I need more light.* Pointing my flashlight beam down, I walk along the length of the boat, searching the water for whatever has drawn the eagle's interest.

I'm almost at the bow when I see a clump of weeds rolled up against the boat at water level. No, wait. It's not vegetation, but a cluster of sea otters rafted together, holding each other's paws. This is often how they sleep. Under my flashlight, pale jowl fur gleams against their darker head fur. Eyes blink up at me, very alert. I almost cover the flashlight, so as to not disturb them, when I recognize what floats in the middle of the group.

"Mackie!"

She's face up, long hair streaming over the otters, her lower body submerged.

I stare in disbelief. Then I run back to the boat ladder, strip to my undershorts, and am in the water swimming to her. The otters watch quietly, as if waiting for me to join them. I don't know what will happen when I reach for her, but when I close in, they ease downward and disappear.

She's not moving. Her face registers blue-white in the dim light. I put my arm around her, and try to find a pulse on her neck. I get nothing. Maybe it's too faint and I'm missing the beat. She remains motionless as I tow her back to the ladder.

Mackie's slack weight is heavy, and I adjust her body so that I have her across my shoulders before I climb the ladder. Because of saltwater in my eyes, I can't see well. It takes a long time to get to the boat rail. Then I give a final push and we both fall on the deck.

She's sprawled in front of me, dead. Inside, I feel as cold as she looks.

I make myself examine her face. Mackie's closed eyes top a calm smile, like she sleeps in the middle of a peaceful dream.

I stagger to the railing and throw up. When I return to Mackie, I hear nothing. Not the sound of the waves lapping against the boat. Not the *ting-a-ling* of the neighbor's wind chime. Not the sound of my own breathing. Everything has gone quiet. Dead quiet.

Chapter 11

I have to do something. I step away from Mackie and go below. Brody hasn't moved. In one of the bedrooms, I find a sheet to wrap around Mackie. Shivering in spasms, I pull out a blanket to put around myself.

Much as I loved Mackie, I don't want to touch her again. When I pulled her out of the water, her skin felt so cold. But rolling her in the sheet seems like the decent thing to do. She probably would like the fabric color. She looked good in lavender.

I turn her so that she faces up into the night sky. Then I place the sheet over her, and tuck it in and under. She has the same serene expression as when I first had hauled her on the boat. I hug the blanket around me and, still watching her, reach for my phone.

As the phone searches for a signal, her eyes open.

My phone clatters as it hits the deck.

"Mackie?" I whisper. "Are you alive?"

She says nothing and doesn't move.

I jump up and watch her with a wild spurt of hope. Next, I run down the cabin stairs and grab the butane lighter. I race back up the stairs to her open eyes that stare straight up into the heavy night sky.

I light the stick and pass it under her nostrils. There's a faint but definite flicker!

"Mackie." I gasp, as I fling the lighter down and touch her face with my hands.

Scrambling, I pick up my phone and dial 911. She will live and I'll see to it!

I put the phone on speaker and tuck my blanket around her as I give information to the emergency dispatcher. The island's fire station is close, and someone should be with us within minutes.

I struggle to pull on my pants over my wet shorts, put on my shirt, and then call my dad's phone. *Please, let him be awake.* He answers before the call goes to voice mail and says to call again as soon as I know which hospital we'll be taken to.

I sit on the deck next to Mackie. *Is she unconscious?* She recovered from a coma after her family's summer sailing accident. But how can she still be alive after being in the water and looking so blue?

How did she end up in the water? And there is the bizarreness of Brody, the eagle, and the otters. How can any of that be explained? It's unbelievable even to me.

When the medics arrive, so does a policeman. He and the EMTs bring high beam lanterns projecting light in fifty-yard paths. The Camerons' property becomes a well-lit stage, and neighbors in pajamas step out of their homes to see what is going on.

The policeman identifies himself as Captain Evans and asks me some questions as the medics attend Mackie and Brody. Captain Evans looks closely at my hands and clothes. He's just placed my shoes, with blood on their soles, in a plastic bag, and is speaking with the EMTs when two more police officers arrive. Officers Dade and Kale size me up like coyotes considering a meal.

When the medics move Mackie and Brody off the boat, I begin to walk with them.

"Stop right now. You're coming with us," Office Kale says.

An EMT replies, "He's been in the water, so we need to check him out. He could have hypothermia."

"He could be dangerous," the cop says.

What? Where is this coming from?

"He was in cold water and could go into shock. One of you can ride in the back with us," says the EMT, who seems to be in charge.

The cop turns to me. "After Harborview, we're going to the First Hill Station. We want a formal statement, pronto."

I have a hard time swallowing.

"You boys have it from here?" Captain Evans asks the cops. He isn't smiling.

"Sure. We've got this," says Officer Kale.

I'm sorry to see the captain move toward his car as I walk between my police escorts. In front of us, Mackie and Brody are carried up the stone pathway to the driveway, and secured in the red and white emergency truck. Officer Dade motions for me to get in. He sits next to me on a narrow bench seat between medical equipment, and places a stun gun on his knee.

I reach in my shirt pocket, show the cop I have my phone, and call my dad.

"Dad, we're going to Seattle. Harborview. Harborview Medical Center. They're getting ready to move us. I'm with Mackie and Brody. Did you call her parents?"

"Yes, we've talked with them. The police are at their place, now. Are you okay?"

"Yeah. I'm fine."

"What about Mackie?"

"She's still not awake."

"Were Brody's parents home?"

"I don't think anyone was in the house."

"Mom and I will meet you at the hospital."

"Okay. Hey, would you bring me some clothes? Mine are kind of wet. I need shoes, too."

"You need to end your call," a medic says, as he sits down between Mackie and Brody.

Then the ER truck's double doors close.

During the ride, Officer Dade keeps his eyes on me and I keep mine on Mackie. Everyone stays inside the ambulance on the ferry.

What went down between Mackie and Brody that she ended up in the water? With a ripped shirt? Mackie breathes through tubes hooked to an oxygen tank. Her eyes have closed and her skin is changing from pale blue to a healthy color.

At 12:47 A.M. Sunday, a Harborview ER tech admits me to be checked out after my cold-water swim. The emergency staff rolls in a wheelchair for me to sit in and asks for my identification information. They've already wheeled Mackie and Brody out of sight, so I don't know anything more about them. Five other people hover in the ER lobby. Two of them look sick and run in and out of the restrooms, another wears a sling on his arm, and the last two just seem sad.

An orderly rolls me down a hallway and into a curtained cubicle. Another man in hospital scrubs with a hospital badge joins us. He says, "Hi. I'm George. I hear you went for a swim in the Sound tonight. Let's get your temperature and blood pressure first." After those tests, he says, "We need to get you warmed up. Take your clothes off and put this gown on." He gestures to a gown lying on an examination table. "I'm going to give you a blanket to wrap around yourself, too."

George pulls a white blanket from an overhead cabinet and sets it next to the gown on the exam table. "The bag on the floor is for your clothes. A doctor will be in to see you, very soon," he says and leaves, pulling the drape closed behind him.

I peel off my clothes and slide into a light-green hospital gown that doesn't really close in the back. After dumping my damp clothes in the hospital bag, I wrap the white blanket with a large tag marked 'thermal' around me, sit on a chair next to the exam table, and wait for the doctor.

I hear Mom and Dad's voices before I see them. When they draw the curtain back to walk in, I notice that Officers Dade and

Kale are stationed outside. *Do they really think I had something to do with Brody and Mackie's being hurt?*

I stand up. Mom hugs me with tears in her eyes, and Dad puts his hand on my shoulder.

"Has a doctor been in?" Dad asks.

"Not yet. A guy took my temperature and blood pressure. I'm fine. Really."

Dad nods. His eyes blink a lot, like they do when he's stressed.

The orderly brings in two chairs. Mom thanks him, and my parents sit down on either side of me. I notice Dad has brought a bag with dry clothes in it.

"Did you run to Brody's house?" Mom asks.

"Yeah. Brody looked really messed up when I found him on the boat. There was a lot of blood. I was trying to find Mackie when I saw her in the water. I thought she was dead." I hope the cops are paying attention.

A man pushes the curtain open, steps inside, and closes the drape behind him. He's about my dad's age, wears glasses low on his nose, and a white lab coat over his clothes.

"Hello, I'm Dr. Sullivan. And you must be Jeremy. I understand you were in the Sound tonight. How long were you in the water and how do you feel now?"

"I feel okay. I think I was in about ten minutes, maybe."

He listens to my heartbeat, asks me to follow a small bright light with my eyes, checks my reflexes, and notes my temperature on the chart.

"Do you have a headache or dizziness?"

"No."

"Since you got out of the water, have you shivered a lot?"

"Yes.

"That's normal. How do your muscles feel?"

"They ache a little."

"Like you could cramp?"

"Yeah."

He makes a note on his tablet.

"Okay. I don't find anything unusual. That's good. But you're going to feel muscle stress from the shivering. Let's get you something to relax. You should feel fine in about twelve hours."

He turns to my parents.

"If he gets a light headache, that's normal. If he's dizzy, that's not. Keep an eye on him."

Dr. Sullivan turns to me. "Okay, Jeremy, you can get dressed now. On your way out, stop by the desk and the nurse will give you a few anti-inflammatory pills. Take one right away and then one every eight hours until they're gone. You're good to go." He heads for the draped doorway, but stops and looks back at me with a grin. "Stay out of the water. Okay?"

Everyone steps outside while I dig into the bag Dad brought. My clean, dry clothes are a reminder of something normal in an otherwise crazy day. When I finish and open the curtain, the police stand talking with my parents at the doorway.

Officer Dade, who sat with me in the ambulance, still doesn't seem friendly. The other cop, Officer Kale, ignores me and speaks with Dad.

"We're taking him to the First Hill Station to make a statement. Maybe he'll be released. Maybe he'll stay. Not our decision."

I look at them in shock. Why would they even think about keeping me? *I saved Mackie and Brody!*

After stopping at the intake desk and taking my pill, I walk out of the hospital between the police. It's a quick drive to the police station. But sitting in the back of their police car, I feel like a criminal. I see my reflection in the passenger side window. It doesn't even look like me. The face I see belongs to some other guy.

At the station, I sit with my parents in a small waiting area until the cops are ready to talk with me. When we're told that my parents can't come with me, my dad insists that an attorney be present before they start any questioning. That is my right, he says. We wait another forty-five minutes until a public defender can be roused from sleep, get dressed, and drive to the station.

That public defender is Ms. Lexa McCarthy. She meets with my parents and me in a small room with one desk and some chairs.

"Jeremy, you won't be able to leave until you make a statement. The police want to know, in detail, what you did tonight. Any information you know that's relevant to Ms. Spence and Mr. Cameron's situation will be helpful. They can't, however, demand answers to questions that you can't answer. If that happens, just say you don't know."

"What if I remember something else later, or get things confused?" I ask.

"You'll get a transcript of the statement to review. You can always make a correction later. Just move at your own pace. Don't let them push you. And I'll be there if you have any questions."

So, while a recorder rests on the table between us, I tell the police about Mackie's lost phone, the search for her, Jilly's call to me, and what I did at Brody's house and on the boat. I leave out a few details, including:

- The eagle that circled over the boat
- The sea otters that formed a floating pillow
- How much Brody's wounds reminded me of an eagle attack

Over an hour later, when I'm ready to drop from exhaustion, the police release me. Just like some words in a crime story, they caution me not to leave the area.

In the parking lot, I ask my parents if we can stop by the hospital to check on Mackie. My dad looks gray-tired. But he says yes.

It doesn't take long to return to Harborview Medical Center. We learn that Mackie is in the Critical Care Unit, and we have arrived after visiting hours. Mom asks if someone will get word to

Mackie's parents that we're in the lobby. In a few minutes, Caitlin Spence approaches us, and throws her arms around me. Tears are in her eyes and running down her cheeks. She thanks me for rescuing Mackie and says I should go up to Room 331; she's cleared it with the nurses.

In the elevator, I feel dizzy. I stumble out and, to steady myself, press my back against the hallway wall. The dizziness stops, and it takes a minute before I find Mackie's room. When I step in the room, Nick Spence grabs me in a bear hug saying "thank you" over and over. At least Mackie's parents don't see me as the bad guy.

Mackie has a room to herself. Her skin color looks healthy again, and she seems comfortable, even with an IV hooked into her arm and an oxygen monitor clipped to her finger. Her dad motions for me to sit in a chair on the other side of the bed, and the two of us watch her.

"Any change?" I ask.

"None. Doesn't mean anything, though. Mac's a little peach pit. She's tough. Four months ago she came out of a coma after a week and was just fine. Jeremy, I'll never in my life be able to thank you enough for going over to Brody's house. She'd be gone. What happened between those two?"

"I don't know. Brody was passed out, so I couldn't ask him anything. He was cut up pretty bad, but it didn't look like something Mackie could have done. Did you get her phone back from the police?"

"No. They're keeping it for evidence. I have my doubts about how much we'll find out through them. You sure gave your daddy a start when you called. He'd been thinking you were asleep in your bed." Nick grins at me.

"Yeah, well, Jilly called and told me that she took Mackie's phone at Kyle's party. Brody took it from her. It didn't sound like Jilly knew Mackie was missing," I explain.

"It wasn't a kindly thing to have done, but this isn't Jilly's fault. Brody's always seemed one shot shy of a full load. Never understood what Mackie saw in him. He's good looking, don't get me wrong there, but he's just so one-dimensional. I was glad when she asked you to the dance. And I sure am happy to be sitting across from you now."

For a few minutes we watch Mackie and listen to the gentle beeping of her vital signs monitor.

I break the silence. "How long do the doctors think she was in the water?"

"That's the odd thing, Bud. Said they had contradictory evidence. Her core temperature was pretty good and so were her vitals, but her skin looked and felt like she'd been in the water for hours. Hours." He shakes his head. "By most counts, she'd be long gone."

"The last time, when she was in the water this summer, did it seem like it was the same?" I pose the question carefully, not wanting to stir up bad memories of their boat capsizing.

"Uh-huh. Very similar. That's why I have so much hope right now. Look at her. She looks good. No damage to anything, not really."

I have one more burning question. "How did she come out of the coma this summer?"

"There's a question you, me, and every doctor would like an answer to. She just woke up one day and could talk and move around almost like it never happened. Other than not remembering the accident, she seemed fine."

That's what I desperately want. For Mackie to come out of the coma like nothing bad has happened. For her to be just fine.

"Ah, the nurse said since this isn't visiting time, I should only stay a few minutes. Guess I'd better be going."

I lay my hand on a part of Mackie's arm that doesn't have needles or tubes. I pat her and silently beg her to wake up. Nick watches and nods.

"You come back, Bud. You're good for her," he says, and there is no doubt in my mind that I've just been given the highest parental stamp of approval that I could ever hope to attain. I only wish Mackie was awake to hear it.

CHAPTER 12

Sunday morning. I sit at the kitchen table with Mom and call Olivia to explain why I won't be in for my afternoon shift at the shelter. She tells me not to worry. She's glad nothing happened to me, and she'll pray for Mackie. I don't argue, but figure that good medicine and rest, not prayer, are what Mackie needs.

My phone doesn't stop ringing. All of our friends want to hear how Mackie is and what happened. Jen tells me that our principal posted a missing child report on the school website after Mr. Spence called him yesterday afternoon. Since then, Mackie's picture has been on all of the social media message boards that parents and kids use. Mackie grew up on the island, so it was scary for everyone to read that she went missing.

Then a call comes through on my mom's phone. Mom hands it to me, saying it's Brody's mother.

"Jeremy, this is Natalie Cameron. Brody's father and I want to thank you. We're waiting for a flight back to Seattle, but I want you to hear this now, from us. We appreciate everything you did. I'm sure Brody will want to thank you when he can."

"Is Brody better?" I ask.

"The doctors tell us he's stable, but he will be in the hospital for a while."

So he came through blacking out from the gin okay. She tells me the police will take his statement at the hospital, and then we say goodbye. *Lucky Brody.* How much does he remember about the eagle? I'd like to be in the room when he explains that one to Officers Dade and Kale.

Early in the afternoon, Wes borrows his parents' SUV and drives Jen, Jon, Erica, and me to the hospital. Just like during the summer when she nearly drowned, it seems weird for us to be together without Mackie.

Wes and I are the first to walk into Mackie's room. His eyes bug out when he sees the tubes hooked into her arms and fingers.

"Oh man, will she get through this?" he whispers to me.

"I think so. She did it once before." If Mackie doesn't come out of the coma, well, I'm not letting myself go there. "I looked 'coma' up. She can hear us, but won't be able to talk or do anything," I say, as we approach her bed.

"Hey, Mackie. We need you to come back from wherever you are. Without you, it's just Ty and me who will have to keep young Jeremy out of trouble. You know how good we are at that." Wes laughs.

I can always count on Wes for humor.

Wes continues. "So, Mackie, you know, you're our alpha survivor. Remember when our tree fort collapsed? You walked away without a scratch. And when Diggy Howard let go of his tennis racket, and it hit your head? Not even a bruise. This coma thing should be nothing for you. And hey, you might miss my latest dance bust-out at Jen's. I know that will be a real disappointment for you, so you'd better come home. Like right now."

I chuckle.

I hold Mackie's hand. There isn't any response, but I want her to know how much I miss her. It's the kind of scene that I would have dismissed as sappy in a movie. That was before seeing her lying in a hospital bed. Now the feelings are so real that it hurts in my bones.

When Wes and I return to the lobby, Jennifer goes up next, by herself, which is fine because Jen has so much energy that she could suck the air out of a room. But not in a bad way. She just has a really big personality. And Jen will focus on Mackie, not all the medical equipment. What most people find uncomfortable is no problem for Jen.

After Jen returns, it's Jon and Erica's turn to go up. They don't stay long and rejoin us surprisingly fast.

"Mackie's doctor came in to check on her. Did Mackie move or do anything when you guys were in her room?" Erica asks.

We shake our heads no.

On the way back to the ferry dock, Jen suggests we stop for something to eat. It sounds good because my appetite has returned. It's like I haven't been able to replace the energy I lost in the cold water fast enough. At least my muscles feel better. Wes tells us it's his treat, and then everyone raises their glass in a salute to me for saving Mackie. I look down in embarrassment. Did I save her, really? She isn't all right.

At home, Mom and Dad talk about how well Justin handled things when they took the ferry to the hospital. He stayed at the Spences' with Noelle so neither of them would be alone that night. Justin woke, climbed in the car, and then fell asleep immediately on the Spences' couch with Noelle on the facing sofa. It's good to have friends.

At home after visiting Mackie, I think about the eagle and the otters. They were there for her. Why? How? What is the connection she has with them?

But these questions don't really matter. What matters is that I need to be with her. That's all I want now. Not to analyze, know, or understand. Just to be with her.

Now, as I crawl into bed at eight o'clock, a full hour and a half earlier than usual, I feel a slight tugging at my skin like something tweaking me, but sleep rolls in like thick fog. I'm gone until my alarm goes off at six thirty.

Monday morning, Ben sizes me up with eyes more serious than usual when I climb in his car to ride to school.

"Is it true what I heard about Brody and Mackie?" he asks.

"Depends what you heard," I reply.

"That Brody was cut up bad, and Mackie's in a coma at Harborview. You found them and called it in."

"Yeah, that's true," I say, watching his face while he drives.

"Well, someone ought to pin a medal on you. Mackie didn't deserve to go through another drowning. Brody, well, life has a way of making a circle."

This is a profound statement for Ben in the morning.

"Yeah, she's still in a coma. Brody, ah, I talked with his mother a little yesterday and he's awake. I'm guessing they have him loaded up on pain meds."

"Oh yeah. I bet he's lovin' that," Ben says.

I'm the object of way too much attention at school today. Everyone wants to ask about Mackie, a few about Brody, and people stare at me wherever I am. It's all too much. I want to go back to being part of the background.

Jen sits with me at lunch and fields most of the questions. At one point even she gets peeved with all the chatter. She throws me a look that begs, 'What next?'

Wes and Ty act goofy like always, and joke about my many newly acquired best friends. At least I can laugh with them about something.

At practice, Coach treats me as if nothing unusual has happened. He reminds me to ease up on the first fifteen minutes of my practice run and push the last five. He mentions Brody indirectly, noting the likelihood that one of our JV runners will move up to run varsity for our next meet.

But in the locker room, the guys have questions.

"Jeremy," Cole calls out. "Word is that you had it out with Brody because of Mackie."

I give him my best you-are-a-dickhead stare.

"Word is wrong. And for the record, Brody would be still sitting on his boat, rotting, if I hadn't gone to his house to find Mackie's phone that he took. So maybe Word should start making corrections about what you just said." I pull my towel out to take a shower. Cole is full of it.

He gives me a shrug.

"That's real nice, Cole," I hear Ben growl as Cole moves past us. *Oh crap, this needs to stop.*

"Okay, I have something to say," I announce, loudly.

It gets quiet. Fast.

"I didn't and don't have it out for Brody. I just happened to be the one who found him and called emergency. I don't know what went down for either Brody or Mackie because neither of them could talk when I found them. Sorry that it's not more juicy, but that's it."

I head to the showers. No one bothers me there.

As I leave the gym, Coach waves me over.

"Mr. Tarleton, you might be wondering whether I reported that little fight you and Mr. Cameron had last week. I did not. Do not make me regret my decision," he says, holding my eyes with an unblinking gaze.

"No problem, Coach," I say, feeling relief.

He nods and says, "There's a saying for what just happened back there, in the locker room. 'No good deed goes unpunished.'"

Coach has that right.

After practice, I ride home with Ben. At dinner, it feels good to sit and listen to Mom and Dad talk about their upcoming week. Mom has spoken with Mackie's mom, who reports no change in Mackie. But in another conversation, Natalie Cameron told Mom that Brody would be sent home soon.

Brody is fine, but Mackie is still in a coma. Of course.

I find it hard not being with Mackie. Other than feeling kind of depressed, the weird thing with my skin continues. The tugging sensation happens more often now. It comes and goes at odd times of the day. Maybe it has something to do with my cold water swim.

By Wednesday, things settle down at school. I can go to class and eat lunch without someone wanting to discuss Mackie or Brody. The rumor that I'm responsible for Brody's injuries has died. At least no one brings it up to me again.

As for Brody, I don't expect to hear from him. Having seen the severity of his wounds I doubt he'll do much of anything for a while. My focus stays on Mackie. I have no sympathy for Brody.

Mackie. *How did she end up in the water?* Other than having hypothermia from being so cold, she has no injuries, no marks that I could see when I pulled her out. That is so different from Brody.

Also, there was the expression on her face when she lay on the boat deck. She'd looked fine, like nothing was wrong, nothing to worry about. None of it adds up.

Friday after school, Wes and Ty attend our home meet set to start at four thirty. All of our school's home meets begin late-afternoon because it takes time for our opponents to reach the island by ferry.

I feel kind of pukey in the locker room before the run, and manage to pull it together when I see Ryan in his pre-race routine, with his earbuds in place, staring into space. This part of my life hasn't changed. It comforts me to see Cole speed-talking as usual, Ethan looking like he might upchuck at any moment, Ben meditating on his feet, and Coach looking like he wants to suit up and run the course himself.

Coach brings us together before the start.

"All right, gentlemen, you have an excellent opportunity to better your times today. We have a light wind out of the south, the temperature is warm enough to run in your T-shirts, and it's dry.

"You have the advantage. You know the ins and outs of this race better than any other guys running on our course today. Stick to your plan. Remember what we talked about on Monday, and how you're going to run. Visualize and make it happen. Now, I want everyone in the box on time and ready for the start. Let's get it!"

We do our team clap and jog, to warm up. My mind lets go of everything else, and I concentrate on how I want to start out slower than usual and pick it up in the middle of the race. That's what Coach has had me working on for the last week and a half. Then I'll kick it at the end.

My plan goes well. I finish eighth and shave ten seconds off my best home time. Ryan takes first and Cole comes in third. Coach jumps up and down at the finish, and our team wins the meet.

After the race, Ty and Wes wave to me, and I walk over to them.

"My man," Wes says. "You kicked butt. I wish you could've seen the guy's face in front of you when you blew by him at the finish. He didn't know you were behind him."

"Seriously," Ty adds.

I'm too tired to say much, but I accept their congratulations with a smile. It felt great to crank myself at the end, like pushing toward something just beyond my reach.

After the meet, I go out for pizza with some of the guys on the team. Since Brody isn't around, the atmosphere feels a lot looser. Or maybe that's just how it feels to me. I'm more optimistic about most things without Brody.

When I walk in the house, it's almost seven o'clock. I find Mom and Dad in the kitchen.

"Would you like to visit Mackie tonight?" Mom asks.

"Yeah, when can we go?"

"Now," she says. She picks up her car keys and asks if I want to drive. As we leave, Dad says to be careful.

I don't get to drive too often because my parents share one car. I almost never drive in Seattle. During the ride to the ferry, Mom asks about my week, but doesn't press.

"It was okay, a little weird at first," I reply. "It's tough because no one knows what happened to Mackie or Brody, and I don't have answers. Some of the guys thought maybe I was the one who hurt Brody."

"What did you tell them?"

"I said I found Brody after he was messed up, and called it in. Since neither Mackie nor Brody could tell me what happened, there wasn't anything else to add."

"Did they believe what you said?"

"Seems like it."

"Natalie Cameron called to say that Brody will go home after he has plastic surgery. And she sounded quite concerned about Mackie, too," Mom says.

"Yeah, I have the impression that Mackie gets along fine with Brody's mom. It's Brody she has a problem with."

"What kind of problem?"

Usually I would have shut up there, but since it's just the two of us, I reply, "He's been bugging her. Like sending messages all the time and claiming that she owes him something. He annoys her. A lot."

"She told you that?"

"Yeah."

"Jeremy, from what Brody's mother said, he doesn't recall what happened to him. He can't remember being attacked, or when you arrived. I think the police may want to talk with you again."

"Why? I didn't do anything to him."

"Of course not, but it's their job to figure out how Brody got hurt. If the police want to see you, we're going to hire an attorney," Mom says.

After driving onto the ferry, we stay in the car. Though the car is in park, I grip the steering wheel anyway. I do not want to deal with Officers Dade and Kale again. It's been clear from the start that they suspect me. If I have to talk with them another time, I will only repeat what I said to them earlier. And according to the

Seattle attorney, Lexa McCarthy, I shouldn't say anything more to them without having a lawyer present.

It's a quiet ride the rest of the way as I reflect on my recent, strange life.

At the hospital, Mrs. Spence meets us in the lobby and stays to talk with my mom while I head to the third floor to see Mackie. In the elevator, the tugging sensation on my skin starts again. This has happened three times in the last two hours. *What's up?*

Mackie looks exactly the same as when I left her on Sunday except that her dark hair is pulled up on top of her head in a ponytail. Her skin color looks perfectly normal, like she might, at any moment, sit up and break out with a laugh and her mischievous sidelong glance.

I sit on a chair close to her bed and stare at her computer monitor. That's when the feeling of something tugging at my skin becomes more like something pulling. *I'm being pulled closer to Mackie!*

As I edge my chair forward, my knees touch the bed rail. I take her hand in mine. She doesn't move. The pressure increases, now from behind. I'm being pushed to lean over her!

I don't know what to do, so I finally stand up and put my hands on her arms, like I'm going to lift her. I start to get the shakes.

Then, just like on the boat, her eyes fly open wide. But this time, she looks up into my eyes, opens her mouth, and says in a voice so clear it could be moving with the current of running water.

"Jeremy."

Chapter 13

On Sunday at noon, two days after she opened her eyes and spoke my name, the hospital discharges Mackie. The doctors kept her the extra days for observation. Since she's been fully conscious and her vital signs and test numbers have stayed normal, they release her with a warning not to overdo things. As her parents and Noelle drive Mackie back to the island, she sends me a message from her mother's phone:

Meet me, 1 hour! My house!

I give it forty-five minutes and run to the Spences' home. When he sees me, Gus bumps his nose against the front window and wags his propeller of a tail. I wait on the porch swing until the Spences' car turns into their drive.

Mackie opens the car door and stands. She looks fine. Better than fine . . . great!

In five running steps I hold her in a hug. When she puts her head on my chest and wraps her arms around me, I have never felt so relieved.

"Mackie, you go ahead now. It's cold out here," Mr. Spence scolds.

Mackie smiles and takes my hand as we walk into the house. Gus somersaults around the hallway corner to reach her side.

Everyone heads for the kitchen. Noelle butts in front of us; then apologizes. Wonders never cease. She asks if we want to watch a movie with the rest of them after eating. Whatever Mackie wants to do is okay with me, as long as we are together. We sit at the kitchen breakfast nook while the Spences place a variety of foods in front of her.

"Stop. Please," Mackie says. "If I eat too much, I'll get sick. Can I have some time to talk with Jeremy? I'm not really up for a movie."

"Mackie, honey," Mr. Spence says. "You're looking like you need to eat. Come on now, I made barbecue last night, all your favorites, and we have leftovers." He waves a drumstick.

"Sure, Dad, I'll eat while I talk with Jeremy. Okay?"

And, with that, we are alone, sitting across from each other at the small table, a plate of warmed barbecue, cole slaw, beans, and biscuits between us.

Mackie puts a finger to her lips and says, "Shhh . . . Mademoiselle Nosy will hear every word. Does my dear sister need something from the kitchen?" she finishes loudly.

Noelle struts in and pretends she needs a glass of water. She nods to both of us and tosses her head on the way out.

"She never stops," Mackie says with a sigh, as she pushes the plate of food to one side.

I reach across the table and place my fingertips against her fingertips.

"Tell me what happened." I say, knowing I shouldn't push since it's her first day back. But I'm beyond asking questions. I need answers to keep me from feeling crazy.

"Yeah. This has to stay between us, okay?"

I frown.

"Promise," she says.

"Yes, I promise."

She takes my hands in hers and holds them on top of the table.

"This is really important. You have to mean it. Like, telling someone what I say could cost you your life." She pauses to gauge my reaction. I lift my eyebrows and nod.

"Brody has wanted to get me away from everyone, and I think I've figured out why."

"What do you mean?" I ask, and lean forward.

She moves her hands from mine and sits back in her chair. Her eyes size me up like she will test me.

Where is this going?

"You know how in science we talk about hypotheticals? You know, a theory that's assumed to exist. Well, let's think of this as a hypothetical situation. So, hypothetically, what if you were right about me being a descendant of Akeso? Let's assume she really lived and her father was Asclepius, the Greek god of medicine. Let's suppose I'm an incarnation or some latest version of her, and this time my name is Mackie. I heal wild animals, and have this connection that allows the animals to pull me to them when one is sick or wounded. 'How?' you might ask."

"Yeah, I'm asking," I barely choke the words out. This is way beyond what I thought she'd say.

"Do you remember the information we read on your computer about Asclepius?"

"I remember some of it."

She pours a glass of water, and sets it in front of me.

"I know this is wild, but stay with me, okay? It's going to make sense," she says.

I put the glass to my lips, not moving my eyes from hers.

"The god Apollo has a son, Asclepius, who becomes the god of medicine. Asclepius marries Epione, and they have children. Akeso is one of them. Like her sisters, Akeso is very good at what she does. She knows how to heal and cure because it's in her genetic code, from Apollo, to Asclepius, to her. Right?"

Mackie stops, pours herself a glass of water, and sips. I gulp at mine.

"As the daughter of a demigod, Akeso finds herself drawn to the sick and wounded. One day, she feels pulled to the shore. She sees a pair of dolphins who float without moving. Akeso dives in and swims to them. She knows that they will live, but she may die. Their healing has been too much for her body."

"Did you read this somewhere?" I ask her.

"No. I'm telling you this because it's something I remembered when I was in my coma in the hospital. Well, let's suppose I remembered. Since it's all hypothetical."

I lean further forward, put my elbows on the table, and cup my chin with my hands. This is some story.

"So Akeso's in the water, dying. After healing the dolphins, she doesn't have enough energy left to swim back to shore. All of a sudden, right in front of her, Poseidon, the god of the sea, appears. He looks at the dolphins and knows that she's the reason they're still alive. And he sees that Akeso won't make it back to the shore.

"Poseidon loves his dolphins. He asks Apollo to save her. Apollo finds a protector for Akeso. His name is Aleksander. Aleksander swims out to rescue her. And he always stays near Akeso, so that he can save her whenever her energy gets too low."

I bite my lip. This is fascinating, but of course it's only a story, maybe a dream or hallucination she had while she was in the coma. There is no way to prove any of it.

"Okay," I say. "I'm following you. But Akeso would have died and so would Aleksander. What makes you think they come back? That they live over and over again?"

"Akeso and Aleksander aren't immortal. They die just like all humans. But she's the child of a demigod and Aleksander's attached to her. They reincarnate almost as soon as they die. Akeso's reborn so she can heal animals. Aleksander comes back to save her if her energy gets low and she's in trouble. Do you see where this is going?"

I shake my head. *Nope.*

"Ah, Jer, you were the one who spelled out Akeso on the Ouija board. How did you come up with that name?"

I open my mouth and close it. I can't answer that question.

"I don't know."

"Yes, you do," she says and waits.

"This is all hypothetical, right?"

"Uh-huh."

"I was thinking of the words you put on the board, *DANGER* and *DARK WATER*. The next thing I knew I picked out the letters for *SAVE AKESO*."

"So there was a connection between all of those words for you?"

"Maybe. But I can't prove it."

She's quiet for a bit.

"Okay, let's talk about what happened on the boat. You know Brody had my phone all the time, right?"

"Yeah, after Jilly called me I figured it out. Brody. What a jerk." I reach for her hands again and she places hers, palms down, in mine.

"Brody knew exactly what he was doing. He took my phone so he could get me alone. He really wanted to hurt me, and used my phone as bait. When I went to his house, I couldn't find him. I waited for what felt like hours. Then, he finally came out of the house and told me my phone was on the sailboat. As soon as we were on the boat, he picked me up and held me out over the side, above the water. I panicked. I could tell he wasn't playing around. He really wanted to hurt me," she repeats, and looks down, seeming to remember how bad that moment had felt.

I nod and hold tight to her hands.

"I was hanging there, over the water, when I saw a shadow. I knew it was an eagle right away, but Brody didn't. At least he didn't look up. When she dove it was beautiful. And awful."

"I could tell an eagle had nailed him," I say. "Remind me to thank Number 26 the next time I see her."

"When she attacked Brody, he dropped me on the deck, and I crawled away from him. He tried to push her off, but she dug her talons in and started using her beak and claws. He couldn't fight her off."

"Yeah, I found him below deck. He was next to an empty bottle of gin. I guess he tried to numb the pain."

"After she finished with him, she flew off. I didn't think he could see, because he had blood in his eyes. I tried to help him sit up, but he threw me against the side of the boat. And that's how I fell in the water."

I pat her hand. I can see how it had all played out.

"It felt just like when our sailboat capsized in June. When I hit the water, I couldn't catch my breath. I think I stopped breathing. Then I felt peaceful. It felt safe in the water, safer than on the boat. There was nothing to worry about. I saw some otters swimming toward me. That's all I remember.

"Maybe I went into the coma then. Whatever was happening to me, or Brody; it all stopped. The next thing I knew, you were above me, looking in my eyes and it was nighttime, but I couldn't say anything."

"That was on the boat deck, after I hauled you out of the water. I thought you were dead. Really. Mackie, you felt so cold, and your skin had turned blue. It was bad."

This time, she pats my hand.

"I'm sorry I scared you," she says. "I wanted to see you again and thank you. I could hear my voice calling your name, but you didn't come. It kept happening before I woke up in the hospital. That was when I felt your hands on my arms, like you would pick me up. You brought me out of the coma. You saved me. Twice."

She holds both my hands, tightly, and I see tears on her cheeks through my own tears. I don't know what to say. All the details of her story make sense, but no sense. I lean over the table and run my hands up over her arms, and then back down to her hands. When I stop, she turns her palms up and I place my hands over hers. Our skin temperatures match. *How do I know that?*

"So why do you think Brody did it? Why did he want to hurt you?"

She gives me a quick grin, like she still has a secret. "You remember I told you that I feel like I know Brody. Better than I know just about anyone." She pauses and frowns. "He's fascinating in a bad way. Like a scary déjà vu. Maybe Brody fits into the reincarnation picture. Do you feel like you know him, too?"

Her explanation makes no scientific sense. I don't trust myself to respond, but shake my head. *No.* I want to bring her back to reality.

"Brody's a crazy dude. That's what I know about him. Can you tell me what it's like to be in a coma?" I ask.

"It's not like being asleep. I couldn't make my body move, but I felt something all the time, and I heard everything people said when they came to visit me. I was so happy the day you came in with Wes."

She pauses, and takes in a deep breath.

"I think there are energy fields around us. Animals use them all the time with each other. It seems to be how they connect with me, too. When I needed you, when I was in the coma, I tried to bring you there, because that's where I was. In an energy field."

"Wow. That's cool. What does that feel like? The energy?"

"There's this light vibration against my skin, like a tugging sensation could start at any minute. It feels good."

I stare at her. The tugging sensation she's described feels like what's been happening to me. *Cool, but weird.*

"I have another question. Why didn't you call me after Brody told you he had your phone? I would have gone to pick it up."

She stiffens a little. "You've done a lot for me already. You shouldn't fight my fights. And Brody feels like a really old fight."

It sounds so reasonable. She's her own person and has always done things for herself. She doesn't want to be a bother. But he tried to hurt her and I would never have let him do that. I'm about to reassure her there is nothing I wouldn't do for her, when Noelle bursts into the kitchen.

"I'm supposed to ask if you're okay," she announces.

"I'm okay," Mackie replies. "We're fine. You don't have to wait. 'Bye," she says, with a shooing motion of her hands.

Noelle turns like a dancer on the ball of her foot, and leaves. Mackie and I stand and she hugs me. The hug goes into my body, and leaves an imprint after she steps away.

"Everything you said, about Akeso and what happened on the boat, I need to think about it. I mean, you're here and that's what's important," I say. I can't tell her how unbelievable her story sounds to me. In fact, it's bizarre and worrisome. *Is Mackie a little crazy?*

She hugs me again. "Okay. But we're good, right?"

"Right."

When she lifts her face for a kiss, I want us to never leave the kitchen, never leave the kiss, and I want to never be without her.

CHAPTER 14

Mackie was right about the new volunteers at the shelter. It didn't take long before one of them decided working a four-hour shift every weekend was not for him. Olivia put Mackie and me back together as the 2:00–6:00 P.M. Sunday crew.

On Sunday, after our shift ends, we walk to my house, eat a lasagna dinner with Mom, Dad, and Justin, and then sit in front of our wood stove reciting our French assignment. Since studying together, my French grammar and pronunciation have improved. But I really want to ask her a question.

"Pardonez, mademoiselle mais, voulez-vous accompagner moi à le Steve Un, s'il vous plaît?" I ask, not looking up from my screen.

She gives her notebook a double take, and then tries to look at my screen. Of course, those words aren't on my screen because I've made them up. Her eyes twinkle as she laughs.

"Mais oui. Certainement," she says. And that is how Mackenzie Allison Spence agrees to go with me to Steve One, our school's 1960s-themed dance where the boys ask the girls.

Sure, there is still unresolved drama over the whole thing with Brody, who hasn't returned to school. On the plus side, Captain Evans made a sworn statement that I had no blood on any of my clothes except for the bottoms of my shoes. That was completely consistent with my statement of what happened when I was on the boat. Eventually, I hope to be ruled out as a suspect.

There's something else, too: My connection with Mackie. I'm getting used to feeling a tug at my skin just before she sends a

193

message or calls. And the idea of energy fields that can be entered fascinates me. From what I've found online, ancient cultures described something similar. And like Mackie, early humans were very tuned into animals. Yeah, maybe there is something to her story. I look forward to exploring that, along with everything else about her.

Of course, I still have loads of questions. Is Mackie a genetic variant, able to survive extreme conditions and connect on an unseen plane with animals? Is she the mythological reincarnation of Akeso, daughter of Asclepius, granddaughter of Apollo, born to heal the sick and wounded? Or is she my childhood friend who trusts me with her innermost secrets, and has more to tell? Maybe she's all of those things.

And if Mackie is Akeso reborn, am I Aleksander, her protector? Will I have memories, someday, of our past lives? I want to believe Mackie, even if I can't prove everything she tells me. To believe her, I have to trust her. One thing I do know: I love her and want to be with her.

So who is Mackie Spence? There's a very good chance we'll figure that out, together.

Epilogue

The Girl

Cool breezes partnered the ascending sun as a young girl ran a maze of uneven dirt trails away from her village. Her destination: a nearby cliff overlooking the Aegean Sea.

The girl had never ventured up the embankment. Nor had she ever dived from the ledge. Today was different. She had to save two dolphins floating in a growing ring of blood.

Gathering courage, she paced back for a running start. Her strong arms pumped as her legs pushed off against the uneven ground. Stones sprayed from the impact of her feet. Black hair flying, she spread her arms like wings as she leapt, diving headfirst. Near the water, she pulled her hands together, and slipped into the waves.

Shocked by the coldness of the water, she kicked to the surface, and found the dolphins.

But they did not respond to her presence. She'd healed animals before, though none this large. The girl worried their wounds were beyond her curative abilities, yet saving them was her mission.

She approached the first dolphin and wrapped her arms around its head. His eyes flickered open, then closed, then opened wide as if he recognized her. Hugging him, she stroked the smooth, soft surface of his sides. As she felt her energy flow to him, her breath came faster and her arms grew tired. After several minutes, he began taking in air through his blowhole. The bleeding under his beak ceased. Their gazes held until he bobbed his head. Then she swam to the second dolphin.

The small female lay flat on the water's surface, her blowhole exposed, but she didn't breathe. The girl followed the same process that she'd used to heal the male.

The small dolphin didn't respond. The girl placed her hands on the skin above the dolphin's eyes and gently lifted. A shudder went through the mammal. The girl treaded water, knowing that hugging this dolphin for support would be too much of a burden. Her gaze never left the dolphin's eyes.

The second healing took longer than the first. By the time the dolphins swam, the girl's hands could no longer push through the water, and she tasted saltwater sliding down her throat. Her energy exhausted, she floated on her back, knowing the tide would carry her away. The dolphins dove around her, welcoming the girl into their family. What of her own father, mother, brothers, and sisters? Would they miss her? Would they be sad when she didn't return home that afternoon? But she had saved the dolphins. There would be honor in her dying. Honor that was worth death.

Apollo's Legacy

Poseidon, god of the sea, rose in magnificence through the water. Bubbles shed from his surface like jewels rolling in sunlight. His eyes narrowed as he viewed the two dolphins leaping joyfully. In the center of their activity floated a girl. With squeals and short staccato bursts of song, the duo lauded her bravery and healing powers. They could save their song. Poseidon knew what had occurred. A rogue shark had attacked the dolphins. The girl had risked her own life to heal his treasures, keeping them from death. And for that, he was determined she would live.

"Apollo," he called out. "Apollo, by all that is good and right, where are you? You have given the world a healer, but she doesn't come equipped with the power to survive. Come, and make this right."

In a flash, the god of prophecy appeared above Poseidon. His eyes shone with irritation at what he interpreted as criticism from the god of the sea.

"Why have you called me here, and in such a lofty tone?" Apollo replied.

"I mean you no offense. Look at her. She is young, a child still. She healed my dolphins at her own risk. That kind of love is rare. Apollo, you have created something brilliant but not finished the job. I'm told that she heals on earth, in the sky, and on the water. Her value to us is already spoken of with regard. Will you not give her aid?"

Apollo looked down at the girl's body. She floated on her back, arms and legs forming an X. Her dark hair fanned in and out around her face, like a sea anemone. The dolphins prodded her with their beaks, trying to keep their healer alive.

As Apollo gazed at the scene, his heart softened. She was lovely. She had her grandmother Coronis' flawless skin and hair. Coronis, the mortal he had loved.

Yes, Apollo knew a part of him was in this divine child. Her ability to heal was a birthright that flowed from him to his son, Asclepius, her father. The girl had inherited her grandfather's healing energy.

"Poseidon, once in a great while you are right," Apollo said. "I shall have to do something, but you know there will be a price down the line. Still, I think I will help her."

As Poseidon nodded his agreement, Apollo looked upon the shore and saw a young boy walking with his dog. The god raised his hand and spoke.

"Protector, you are needed." No sooner did Apollo make this proclamation than the boy began running to the shoreline. The girl's protector was on his way.

The Protector

She felt his hands on her shoulders before she saw him. "Don't be afraid," he said. "I saw you in the water. It didn't look like you would make it out by yourself."

They were on the beach of the cove, under the warm rays of the afternoon sun. He sat in front of her, frowning his concern.

"Aleksander," she whispered, willing her eyes to fully open. He lived in her village and they had played together as young children. But lately he attended school with his older brothers. This year, she had seen him only when she walked on the beach with her family.

"I must thank you," she said, struggling from weakness to get the words out. He waved a hand. It was nothing.

"What made you go out so far?" he asked.

This time she searched his curiosity-filled eyes before answering. How much had he seen? His calmness suggested he knew nothing of the dolphins and the healing. She relaxed.

"I misjudged my strength," she said. "How long has it been since you pulled me out of the water?"

"Not long, maybe a half hour. You were turning blue."

"May I ask how you saw me in the water?"

"Oh, I was walking with Archer," he nodded to his dog. "I saw you right away. I thought you had already drowned. But what if you were still alive? Perhaps it was both our fates to be here today."

"Then I am the lucky one, for your fate held mine. Please, would you help me up?"

Aleksander stood and held his hand out to her.

"I must return home. And you will have questions, too, from your family if you are late."

"Oh, don't worry. My parents are used to me losing track of time. I love the beach. There is so much to do here. I thought you were a sea goddess," he smiled and his white teeth flashed against his bronze skin.

She froze and looked so shocked that he laughed. "Well, I can dream, can't I?" he said as they started up the winding path leading away from the beach.

Asclepius, God of Medicine

The girl had been summoned to the porch of her home. She stood before her father, Asclepius, wise god of medicine.

"Daughter," he greeted her, as he moved among his pots of rosemary, thyme, frankincense, coriander, and mandrake. "Let us sit and speak of your latest healing, of which I have heard glowing reports."

She looked up at him. Until that moment, she had worried about his response to her healing animals instead of humans.

"I understand that your grandfather has given you a protector, to keep you from harm when you overspend your energies. That is quite an honor. You must have greatly impressed him."

"Father, I am humbled. My skills are not so great. I was able to heal two dolphins, but couldn't return to shore by myself. I did not know my rescue today was Apollo's will."

"Apollo always has you in his heart. Do we know the boy who helped you?"

"He is Aleksander, of the house of Nikos. You have met him. He pulled me from the water."

"You should know that Aleksander is with you now and forever. By Apollo's wish, your fates have twined together and you must care for him as he cares for you. Do not ask more of him than his abilities allow. He cannot help you heal, only prevent you from dying young."

"When will I have full power?"

"I do not know. Your brothers and sisters have achieved greatness at different ages. You may, in time, heal very large beasts or many at one time. This will take an extraordinary amount of energy, beyond what you can provide today."

"What should I do for now, when I am compelled to heal that which is beyond my strength? What if I must heal two more dolphins tomorrow?"

"Then your protector will hurry to your side and retrieve you, that you may refresh your vital energies out of harm's way. Now, come. Let us thank my father for providing you with Aleksander."

The girl and her father directed words of praise and appreciation to Apollo for his greatness.

Zeus' Judgment

When Hades, the god of the underworld, was upset, his mood ranged from stormy gray to deepest black. This day the lower realm quaked.

"The gods of the sea and of prophecy have gone too far!" he thundered. Pacing in his dark den, Hades grew more and more angry.

"Zeus!" he called out. "First, Apollo creates his son, the healer Asclepius, who interferes with Death. Now, he recasts fate when he alters his granddaughter's path to my door. And Poseidon bid Apollo to save her! What gives them the right to snatch those destined for my gates? What allows Apollo to create a boy-protector, saving the girl from certain death? I demand justice."

He continued thundering until Zeus responded.

"Hades, my brother, you will have your wish. I, too, would like to understand their actions. I call upon my fellow Olympians to hear of this matter."

The twelve major Greek gods and goddesses assembled at Zeus' home on Mount Olympus. It was the first time in many years that Hades had left his underworld to sit with them.

"My greetings to all," said Zeus. "Hades, as Keeper of the Dead, claims that Apollo and Poseidon have rearranged the natural order. That they deprived him by saving a dying girl from her fate and have granted a mortal the status of protector, that she and he may never reach the underworld. Poseidon, Hades believes you encouraged this scheme."

Poseidon stood immediately to speak, trident at his side.

"We have reason to rejoice," he began. "Today a great tragedy was averted. My beloved dolphins, that bring me messages and cheer me with their companionship, were wounded. The girl, Apollo's granddaughter, a healer with his energy in her, saved them but would have died herself if he hadn't interceded. Apollo gave a mortal boy the status of protector to her, that she may continue her good works.

"What if, instead of the dolphins, they were your animals: the owl, the eagle, the deer, the crow—yes, Hades, the crow—who had been dying? Would you reward their healer with death for saving your companions?

"Apollo's son, Asclepius, the healer taught by Chiron, is the girl's father. She is still young and doesn't have her full powers. Yet she saved my dolphins. Such noble courage should be commended. How can we do otherwise?"

Only Artemis, goddess of the hunt and Apollo's sister, looked on with sympathy.

"Apollo, what is your response to Hades' accusations?" Zeus asked.

Apollo's handsome face showed no concern as he stood in splendor, the light of the sun radiating from his being.

"The girl will, of course, die. However, because her existence is tied to me she can never be claimed by Hades at his gates."

The Olympians leaned forward with interest.

"Because her father Asclepius is my son, her life force comes from mine. Therefore, she will never meet Hades in the underworld. Her fate is to live infinite lifetimes, curing the sick and wounded. So Hades' objections are irrelevant. He has no claim to her soul.

"As to the protector, he has no status other than to appear next to her when she needs aid. He cannot heal. His service is to retrieve her when her energies become depleted, that she may continue her work on our behalf in any one of her lifetimes."

Each member of the tribunal nodded except for Hades, who abruptly drew to his feet.

"Wonderful speech, Apollo. Just wonderful. But you're forgetting one thing: it was your own folly that created Asclepius and his spawns. Now you grant them immortality? That goes against our laws. Only we, the high gods and goddesses, may remain immortal. Zeus, shall Apollo be absolved for what he has done?"

Zeus raised his hand, signaling his understanding of the issues.

"Hades, Poseidon, and Apollo have stated their views and concerns. Hades, my brother, as the god of darkness will you accept my decision as supreme in this matter?

Hades did not object.

Zeus continued, "For any child of a god, rebirth is a birthright. And so it is true also for their children. For that reason, the children of Asclepius, son of Apollo, are not destined for the underworld. That includes the girl who was saved today. She will be reborn with her healing powers intact each time she meets with Death."

Hades' harsh breath shook the room. Zeus, a commanding presence among his fellow gods, directed waves of calm to his brother. Hades' breathing slowed and order prevailed.

"Still, Hades, you have given us something to think about. Apollo has granted another, not of his line, status to die and be reborn as protector to the girl."

Zeus paused and looked at Apollo and then at Poseidon.

"Apollo, I will allow it this time, because I believe your intentions were pure and you meant no offense to Hades. Poseidon, I believe you also meant only goodness in your advice to Apollo. Let us view this outcome as a benefit to all of our realms."

The gods and goddesses nodded at Zeus' judgment. Hades scowled, and withdrew to his underworld.

Hades' Revenge

After meeting at Olympus with the gods and goddesses, Hades returned to his world below ground, vexed. Zeus' decision had usurped his authority as Lord of the Dead. Zeus was the arbitrator, but his ruling was not just. And Apollo, that peacock of the sun, had spoken in such an insulting manner.

Furious, Hades considered calling for the Erinyes. The three Furies had avenged him many times, torturing the lives of mortals who murdered each other and deprived Hades of death's natural order. But this assignment required a far broader reach than their powers.

He sat for several days, lost in deep thought. His pride had been wounded by Apollo's actions and condescending attitude.

Hades reasoned, "Apollo has provided a protector for the girl. Let's see how good a protector he can be. I shall provide an agent to test his, and her, mettle. Perhaps the protector and girl will live long and fruitful lives. Perhaps not."

Dismas

Aleksander ran, laughing, to the beach with his two friends and their dogs. The weather was hot and dry, a perfect afternoon for swimming and diving from the rock cliff.

He thought about what had happened the day before, how he'd rescued the girl. He'd never swum out so far before. His older brothers had warned him to stay close to the shoreline. The pull of the tide could be dangerous. Still, he'd been able to push her toward the shore ahead of him, kicking with his strong legs and feet at the water.

"Last one in is a rotten fig!" yelled Mentes, as he dashed past Aleksander and Philetor.

"Right. Prepare to rot!" Philetor retorted as he sprinted after Mentes.

Aleksander grinned, knowing he could outrun both of them. Today, it didn't matter. He'd proven himself yesterday, though he had not said a word about saving the girl to anyone. He kept silent, as if the rescue should remain just between himself and the girl.

A little later, the boys hiked up the slope that led to the diving ledge. Aleksander dove first, accurately throwing himself into a deep section of water. He bobbed up to see Mentes, and then Philetor, dive and surface near by. The three boys swam to the beach, splashing each other on the way.

As he blinked from the saltwater in his eyes, Aleksander saw Archer in a stiff-legged pose. Archer's ears were flattened back as he growled at Dismas, a boy from their village.

"Ho, Archer," Aleksander called to get his dog's attention. Archer didn't back down.

"Sorry," Aleksander, called out. "He's never acted like this before. Usually he's so friendly he won't stop licking your hand."

"He's a dangerous dog. If he bites me, both of you are dead meat," Dismas snarled.

Aleksander and his friends stared at Dismas as he made his way up to the diving ledge. What had just happened? Aleksander patted Archer, but the dog vigilantly watched Dismas climb the embankment.

Artemis Warns Apollo and Alerts Zeus

Artemis didn't like what she'd seen. After the group meeting at Olympus, she caught up with her brother, Apollo.

"What was that about?" she asked, throwing an arm around him affectionately.

Apollo kissed the top of his sister's head. He loved her, but she worried too much.

"I knew it was risky to make the boy a protector. But Poseidon agreed with me that the girl will need someone. I can't always be there for her."

"I understand, but Hades didn't take it well. He stared ten kinds of wrath at you after Zeus made his ruling. What makes you think he won't retaliate?"

Apollo shrugged. "These are small matters for the ruler of the underworld to trouble himself about. Are you worried he will come after me? Let him try." Apollo flexed his biceps and laughed.

"Oh, my brother, do not underestimate Hades. He won't pick a fight with you. He has other ways of getting even when he feels disrespected."

Apollo considered his sister's words.

"He would have to go against Zeus, and that could be a disaster for everyone," he said.

"Exactly."

"Well, we will see. I haven't heard from Hades since he left. Be optimistic. I like you best when you smile."

Grimacing, she shook her finger at him, but kissed his cheek as a goodbye.

Leaving her brother, Artemis considered her options. She could do nothing, and see what happened. Maybe Apollo was right and Hades had no time to spend on revenge. Or, she could watch over Hades herself. But that would be impossible. Hades would feel her presence. No, she would go to Zeus with her concerns.

Entering Olympus, she marveled as always at the beauty of Zeus' house. The temple-like façade with stone columns was lit by a golden sun in an azure sky. Grapevines provided cover above open-air porches, and olive trees offered a fragrant scent.

Zeus greeted her from his lofty perch. She presented him with a stag for his banquet.

"Artemis, thank you for such a bountiful gift," Zeus said. "What brings you to my house again so soon?"

"Concern for the situation that was last discussed."

"Ah, the spat between my brother and your brother. It may come to naught. I have faith that Apollo has given the boy-protector survival skills. This protector already saved the girl in treacherous water."

"He's just a boy. What if Hades sets some demented soul upon him? How could he, or the girl, cope with a wraith from the underworld?"

"Oh, Hades knows better, and he is capable of restraint. However, your warning does not fall on deaf ears. Hades has two sides, light and dark, both of which I am well aware. I will look in on the situation from time to time."

Artemis thanked Zeus, and bid him goodbye.

Zeus sighed. He did not wish to further irritate Hades. Perhaps he'd have a word with Hades' wife, Persephone. No, that would only upset her mother, Demeter, again. Such complex family politics. The boy-protector and the girl-healer would have to take care of each other.

A Taste for Revenge

Aleksander hadn't seen the girl for several weeks. Summer had drawn to an end when he chanced upon her, as he carried a jug of water from the village well.

"Hello. How are you on this day?" he asked.

"Very well. And yourself?" she countered.

"Been swimming lately?" he responded, trying to suppress a grin.

"No. Have you rescued any half-drowned goddesses lately?"

"Goddesses, mortals, I'll save them all. You know, you really weren't all that heavy."

"I'm big enough," she answered with a mock pout.

They continued together on the pathway leading back to their homes. Archer ran ahead, frisking as he caught scents of cats and other dogs. Aleksander and the girl didn't see him suddenly shift into a low crouch and growl.

Dismas stood in a doorway as the trio passed, covertly watching the girl and Aleksander. His heart filled with a volume of darkness that he could not understand. He didn't really know either of them that well, not enough to explain this overwhelming antipathy. But he could not deny the rage he felt. It left a bitter taste in his mouth. A bitter taste for revenge.